Praise for Jack Pendarvis

"At once the funniest and saddest thing I've ever read…. You laugh at what's on the page; you're haunted by what's not…. Pendarvis isn't afraid to let [humor] seep into his stories to mingle with the poignancy and poetry there…. In the end, all these stories are un-failingly kind to their characters and respectful of their cracked dreams. Pendarvis' people want to be noticed, they want to be heard, they want to be recognized as special. In other words, they're human. Only funnier." —Laura Lippman, *New York Times* bestselling novelist, on NPR

"Since the great Pryor and his multiple imitators I have pined for a genius who could stand and deliver equal wit and riot in any guise. Jack Pendarvis is the answer to that prayer…. Thank God Pendarvis, very Southern, is regionless because of his genius for language. The flabbergasted pilgrim, pedant, or loser has never been better done." —Barry Hannah, author of *Geronimo Rex* and *Airships*, in *The Oxford American*

"I would characterize him as a dangerously funny writer: his gaze doesn't flinch when he looks at his characters, but throughout it also maintains an essential kindness. Risky, courageous stuff. Suffice to say, I'm a fan." —George Saunders, author of *In Persuasion Nation* and *Tenth of December*

"Pendarvis is a gifted, good-humored writer. He's wry…his language full of provocative puns, eloquent blarney, and tips of the hat to the absurdity of modern culture. At his best, he is neo-Chaucerian. If you're game, he'll show you a rude, jolly time in a universe at once fantastic and familiar." —*New York Times Book Review*

Movie Stars

Also by Jack Pendarvis

The Mysterious Secret of the Valuable Treasure

Your Body Is Changing

Awesome

Cigarette Lighter

Movie Stars

Stories

Jack Pendarvis

DZANC BOOKS

DZANC BOOKS

5220 Dexter Ann Arbor Rd.
Ann Arbor, MI 48103
www.dzancbooks.org

Library of Congress Cataloging-in-Publication Data

Names: Pendarvis, Jack, 1963- author.
Title: Movie stars : stories / by Jack Pendarvis.
Description: First Edition. | Ann Arbor, MI : Dzanc Books, 2016.
Identifiers: LCCN 2015033335 | ISBN 9781938103452 (paperback)
Subjects: | BISAC: FICTION / Short Stories (single author). | FICTION / Humorous. | FICTION / Occult & Supernatural.
Classification: LCC PS3616.E535 A6 2016 | DDC 813/.6--dc23
LC record available at http://lccn.loc.gov/2015033335

Some of these stories have been published elsewhere, often in very different forms and with different titles: a portion of "Cancel My Reservation" in *The Atlantic*; "Detective" in *Lent*; "Duck Call Gang" in *McSweeney's*; "Encouragement," "Mississippi River," and "Wheelbarrow" in *The L.A. Review of Books*; "Frosting Mother's Hair" in *Knee-Jerk*; "Ghost College" in *The Oxford American*; "Jerry Lewis" in the anthology *Mississippi Noir*; "Joan Crawford: A Hot-Looking Woman" in *Real Weird*; "Pinkeye" in *Pleiades*; "Taco Foot" in *Smokelong Quarterly*; "Texaco Sign" in *This Land*; and "Your Cat Can Be a Movie Star!" in *Cedars*.

Account of a deadly house fire taken, occasionally verbatim, from the Mobile, Alabama, *Daily Register* of January 18, 1885, though details have been greatly changed and the characters are, of course, fictional, with no relation to the actual victims. A few brief phrases, clearly indicated within the text, are quoted from an actual auction catalog, *Property from the Estate of Bob & Dolores Hope*.

First US edition: April 2016
Printed in the United States of America

10   9   8   7   6   5   4   3   2   1

Contents

GHOST COLLEGE   3

PINKEYE   19

JOAN CRAWFORD: A HOT-LOOKING WOMAN   27

JERRY LEWIS   29

CANCEL MY RESERVATION   35

FROSTING MOTHER'S HAIR   73

YOUR CAT CAN BE A MOVIE STAR!   85

MARRIAGE   111

TACO FOOT   113

TORNADO   117

DETECTIVE   119

DAZZLING LADIES OF SCIENCE FICTION   123

APPENDIX: HURT'S NAPKIN STORIES   133

THE BLACK PARASOL   135

ART IS THE MOST IMPORTANT THING   163

DUCK CALL GANG   165

For Theresa
…and the members of Good Idea Club:
Jimmy, Lizzie, Brendan, Liam, Bill, and McKay

In the neighborhood of Leeds there is the Padfoot, a weird apparition about the size of a small donkey, "with shaggy hair and large eyes like saucers"…to see it is a prognostication of death.

T.F. Thiselton Dyer, *The Ghost World*, 1893

Movie Stars

Ghost College

1

IN SHORT, EXPLAINED THE TELEPHONE VOICE OF THE SOOTHING woman, very little work, a nice salary, freedom, a place to live, all bills and expenses taken care of invisibly by invisible hands. There were no strings. She reiterated that he would be required to teach just one class of his own devising per semester.

"My own devising, huh?" said Cookie. It sounded like a trick.

"The Fellowship is designed to give you maximum time to work on your own projects, whatever they may be. You're familiar with the composer Sir Robert Mandala? Best known for his 1965 symphonic suite *Six Hypnagogic Pieces*? The score famously included instructions for putting the orchestra into a trance prior to each performance, an anomaly in his catalog, an early experiment, yet it drew us to Sir Robert and his work. Sir Robert chose to spend his term as a Woodbine Fellow finishing his long-awaited opera *Benedict Arnold*, an earthy subject, you might say. He dedicated the score to us."

"That's nice."

"Yes, an honor. So, as you can see, the personal work in which he was engaged during his term was not about conventionally paranormal subjects, despite the interests of the school. He enjoyed complete freedom and so will you. Incidentally, Sir Robert was so inspired by our students and our program here that he decided to compose his next opus on the subject of the yeti. As you can see, then, the relationship was mutually beneficial. Sir Robert had been stuck on the last act of *Benedict Arnold* for thirty years prior to his acceptance of the Fellowship. We restored his creativity. Sir Robert, when last heard from, was hiking into the Himalayas at the age of nearly eighty."

"That's great," said Cookie.

"He was never seen again."

"Oh, that's bad," said Cookie.

"The premiere of *Benedict Arnold* was given in Fort Worth, where it received stellar reviews."

"That's good," said Cookie.

"But the composer was not there to hear it. He is missing and presumed dead, of course."

"That's too bad," said Cookie.

"We were drawn to you initially because of your marvelous novel *Look Behind You*. Our board believes it shows extraordinary sensitivity to matters supernatural."

"Oh, that was a novelization," said Cookie.

The woman asked what a novelization was and Cookie had to tell her in so many words that it was hack work so some corporation could make a few more pennies off a movie, and that the few people who had bought his mass-market paperback novelization of *Look Behind You* did so because Tommy Lee Jones was on the cover. It had nothing to do with Cookie's so-called talents, except for meeting deadlines, of which he was the king. He could say that for himself.

Later, Cookie's wife came home.

Cookie's wife smelled so good, like a flower smoking a cigarette. She gave off warm waves. Cookie liked it when she leaned in and whispered. She always had a fever. She was a nature poet with super-powers brought on by her constant fever—a well-known nature poet who should remain anonymous here.

"Well, we're moving to Mississippi and I'm going to teach at a ghost college," said Cookie.

"Okay," said his wife.

Cookie liked his wife. She was up for anything.

"I'd love to stop writing about pies for a living," Cookie said.

"You don't have to convince me. And you've got that thing you've been wanting to work on."

"That thing has ceased to interest me."

"Maybe it will start to interest you again. Or maybe you'll get a new idea."

"A new thing," said Cookie.

"A new thing," said his wife.

They clinked imaginary glasses. Ghostly glasses!

2

It was in a snug loft above an unpromising dentist's office that Cookie took up his residence at the ghost college. There was no TV. A large, iconic white tooth, made of plastic and lit from within, shone under the bedroom window, and as Cookie and his wife would soon discover, it was never turned off.

During the day, when Cookie was trying to write, came the whine of the drill and the screams of little children.

Some fifteen years before, when the space, upstairs and down, had been occupied by a renowned doll hospital, an extraordinarily cruel murder—never solved—had occurred in the very loft where Cookie and his wife now lived.

The generally sullen and mostly demure student who had shown them around upon their arrival, a young woman with bangs and cat-eye glasses, told them with an inappropriate burst of open delight how the killer had pooped on the floor.

It was hard to sleep that night. Cookie's wife tried to distract him with a loose floorboard. "Listen, it makes a donkey sound," she said. She demonstrated. The loose floorboard made a *hee* when she stepped on it and a *haw* when she lifted her foot.

Cookie was amused, but it proved a vague and temporary amusement.

"This is all my fault," he said.

By now his wife was sitting at the little desk, working on a poem about the floorboard. Look at her. She was a visionary. A poem about a floorboard!

"Why are we here?" Cookie said. "Where there's no TV? What am I going to do without TV?"

"Write," said the nature poet.

"How did we get shut up in this little place in the middle of nowhere with the stench of death all over it?"

But it did give Cookie an idea for a first sentence: "The murder house had been turned into a bed and breakfast."

He imagined a big old Victorian house in the flat middle of Indiana: back in Victorian times, a man in a velvet suit had lived there and smothered his visitors with a special pillow. A hundred years later, a woman inherits the house from a distant relative she never knew she had.

But there's a caretaker who dresses up as the murderer and gives tours. Teenage girls want him to take their pictures as they lie in the murder bed and he holds a pillow menacingly over their heads. He comes to the gymnasiums of their schools and gives lectures in character:

"Do I appear familiar? I invented a tonic that is still in use today. My talents include playing the harpsichord and adeptness at spontaneous rhyme. I owned a rather famous pet raccoon named Nero. Before the days of my more unpleasant notoriety, my raccoon was written up in *Collier's* magazine as perhaps the largest domesticated specimen in existence at that particular moment in American history, though it must be admitted that raccoons in general were smaller then. How I envy your twenty-first century its healthy and enormous raccoons!

"I am credited with inventing the saying 'Somebody pinch me' to express a surprise so very pleasant that one feels one must be dreaming. In 1892, I was put on trial for murder. Here in your twenty-first century, many people believe that I did not murder anyone. Others put the estimate at seventeen. My name is William Butter.

"I, William Butter, died in my own bed. I was never convicted of any crime. When my body was found, my hair had turned completely white. Just the day before, witnesses had referred to it as 'a healthy chestnut in coloration.' Yet at the moment of my death, even my pubic hair turned white."

The students laughed and the teachers had to quiet them down.

"And whiter than snow was my fine and luxurious mustache, formerly a source of constant pride. Some say it was my downfall, my famous pride. Others say that I did not have a downfall. On my death certificate, in the space provided for cause of death, the coroner made the unusual notation, 'No cause.' Why he did so is a mystery to this very day. But my humble existence was not always gloomy for me. I lived during an exciting period in our nation's history. I had adventures and fell in love. This is my lively story."

———

3

An abandoned playground is a gothic wonder, especially with frost on the ground and a lone grown man sagging in the saddle of a swing. Now imagine that the chinless, pale man, with teeth that stick out a little under an elaborate ginger moustache, has pale bulging eyes and holds to the chains of the swing, motionless. And now imagine him wearing a suit of plum-colored velvet and the soft white rabbit-skin gloves of a murderer. A purple silk top hat rests on his lap. His walking stick leans against one metal leg of the swing set's frame. His overshoes and pant cuffs are covered in a greasy black slime that glitters with speckles of frost. The few slim trees are black and bare.

"Is this swing taken?"

Stanley turned his big, sad head and saw a girl.

"Not at all," he said.

"Not at all!" said the girl. "I like the way you talk. Like a movie where people wear clothes."

"Should you be speaking to a stranger?"

"I'm sixteen," said the girl. "I'll be sixteen soon. Legally, I can talk to whoever I want. My parents live overseas for some reason."

"I'm not comfortable talking to you," said Stanley. "Let's just sit quietly in our separate swings."

"Wait, who are you being?"

"What do you mean?"

"I'm fourteen," said the girl. "I'm telling you because you probably figured it out already. Don't you recognize me?"

Stanley didn't look at her. He rubbed his nonexistent chin with his soft glove. He had not arranged for transportation because Jane Abbott, the new owner of Butter House, was supposed to meet him here. He had expected to ride back with her. But she was almost an hour late and there was no way to get in touch with her.

"I was in the class today," the girl said. "So I couldn't be sixteen. I thought you were really good today and informative about interesting subjects. That's why I asked you who you're being. Like, am I talking to William Butter right now?"

"No," said Stanley.

"Could I?"

Stanley looked at her. She was a kind girl with a plump, chapped face. Her lips were shiny from an application either medicinal or cosmetic. Her hair was straight and gave the impression that she did not care about it one way or another. She wore a leather jacket with numerous attachments. Her nails were painted a very dark red. She wore a lot of rings that looked like tin or plastic, and the cat-eye glasses of a bygone era. She seemed harmless, or at any rate an improvement over the rough boys who had tricked him into stepping into the slippery, sinking patch of black grass in which the school's septic tank was acting up.

"Did you have an interest in William Butter before my performance today?" he said.

"No, do it as William Butter," said the girl.

"Have you long entertained an interest in my person?"

"That is so cool."

"Cool in what manner?" said Stanley as William Butter. "I am not acquainted with this usage of the word."

"So, like, what's it like to smother somebody?" said the girl.

"I cannot say."

"You cannot say or you will not say?"

"A fascinating distinction, yet I must leave your curiosity unsatisfied. In the time period and social milieu I occupy, it is most improper for a young lady to speak of such ghoulish fancies."

"I wonder what it's like to get smothered," said the girl.

"I am no longer William Butter," said Stanley. "I am back to being myself. I don't wish to continue this conversation, I'm sorry."

Cookie was basing the curious girl on Cat-Eye Girl, the student who had shown them around.

In the end, our heroine, Jane Abbott, discovers that William Butter, her ancestor, was innocent. A guest high on laudanum had fallen into a drowse, allowing Butter's large raccoon to rest on his face, resulting in suffocation. William Butter was so dedicated to his raccoon that he refused to incriminate it, fearing that it would be euthanized.

Writing from a woman's point of view was going to rejuvenate Cookie's spirit and stop him from being a hack. It was going to unleash his genius. But the pie company called in need of an emergency supplement. Cookie tried to tell them he was through with pies for good, but they said, "Nobody writes about pie the way you do." They said, "I don't even *like* pie anymore, and you make me like it with your words." They offered to pay him more. Cookie said all right. He didn't tell his wife because it was shameful and desecrating, like committing adultery with the pie company.

At some point they stopped paying him with money and started paying him in pies. Cookie hid the boxes from his wife and ate the pies in the middle of the night while she slept. They had a weird aftertaste, like dust.

4

Cookie ended up calling the class he taught "The Art and Science of the Ghost Story," which meant nothing. It met on Tuesdays and Thursdays for an hour and fifteen minutes.

The first day was easy. Cookie went around the room asking each of his twelve students to describe the last ghost he or she had seen.

There was a sad old man who stood at the foot of a bed.

There was a blue light that floated around.

There was a kindly woman who sat on the edge of a bed.

"I haven't seen a ghost since I was a kid," said this one kid, this kid named Dennis Guy.

"Do you remember it?" said Cookie.

"Aw, *hells* yeah," said Dennis Guy. "It was this shadow man. He looked like a shadow, and he lived in the wall of my bedroom. And he had these ten little shadow monkeys who would help him."

"Shadow monkeys?" said Cookie.

"They were these little shadows about the size of a spider monkey, and they hopped around like monkeys. One night, I left a plate of food on my dresser, and the shadow monkeys came out of the wall and ate it."

"Now, see, that just sounds crazy to me," said Cookie.

The class was taken aback.

"Hey, you think this is bad?" asked Cookie. "I should tell you about the time I made an old lady cry."

The students didn't seem interested.

"I called her at home later, to apologize. Her husband said she had 'taken to bed with a little brandy.' That's what he said! 'Taken to bed.' He said, 'a little brandy.'"

The students still didn't seem interested.

"It was a fiction writing class, the place where I made her cry, the old lady. I had her in an archery class, too. Once she said, 'The arrows make such a lovely plop when they hit the target.' Lovely plop."

He looked at them. He couldn't tell whether they understood that "plop" was the wrong word. So was "lovely." So was the combination "lovely plop." He supposed it didn't matter.

"I don't care," said Dennis Guy. "I don't care if you believe me or not. This isn't what I want to do anyway. I plan to wear a turban and go around reading rich socialites' minds. And then when I get enough money I'm going to go out where there are actors and be an actor."

The kid had the looks for it. He was a bland kid with steely blue eyes and steely blue stubble.

"Okay, great. Hey, is there an old graveyard around here? Wouldn't it be fun if we met in an old graveyard? I think class should meet in an old, abandoned graveyard."

It was Cookie's last idea.

5

The town was nice anyway. There was a rare old family called the Crowns. They were seven sisters with captivating eyes and long white hair pulled back, strong, beautiful, athletic women who gardened, all in their sixties or early seventies, blessed with glowing complexions, the radiant Crowns, ageless goddesses of Mississippi.

Each Crown sister was married to a prominent local gentleman—the sheriff, for example. An obstetrician. The town historian. A guy who owned buildings.

Each of the seven husbands had a different surname—Melvis, Ronson, Turner, Blot, Garland, Chesterfield, Mayhew—but all of them were thought of as Crowns.

Cookie loved the Crown sisters. They held the ghost college in disdain and merrily encouraged him to gossip about it. He would go to their houses and sit in chairs overlooking their gardens and drink cold martinis as the sun went down. He imagined himself into the peaceful existence of a country squire.

"I can do what I do from anywhere," he said.

"Nothing?" said his wife.

"Yes, I can do nothing from anywhere."

The Fellowship had all but expired, and it was time to pack up and return to their penthouse in the big city. Cookie didn't want to go.

"You're a nature poet," he said. "Don't you want to live in nature?"

The nature poet explained that nature is everywhere and she wanted to live in her luxurious penthouse, near her friends and surrounded by her worldly possessions. But Cookie was on the verge of that new thing, he said, that famous new thing.

He had made a mistake, secretly keeping up his pie assignments at the expense of his popular murder novel.

After his wife went back to the city for good, leaving Cookie behind, he occupied himself mainly with old movies and drinking.

He was so glad to have a TV again. When he didn't have one, he thought about it every day.

"I wonder what's on TV right now," he would say.

"You can watch TV on the internet," his wife told him.

"It's not the same," he said. "I'm old."

The morning she left to go back to the city, she dropped by Cookie's new place on her way out of town. He showed her all the musty furniture with which the house had come furnished and the place where the TV would go.

"You don't have to pay for one. It's a waste. You should just come get ours," she said.

"But it's not a flatscreen."

"So what? It has a nice big screen."

"It's shaped differently than TVs are shaped now. To have one in your home is kind of like walking around in…what's something unfashionable to walk around in?"

"A burnoose," said the nature poet.

"Yeah," said Cookie. "And when you watch the square TV, the sides of all the new shows are cut off. Like maybe there are people standing off to the side of the stage doing funny stuff on *Saturday Night Live*, and I can't see them. Sometimes I see a shoulder or a hand on the edge of the screen and wonder what I'm missing. On the other hand, I like old movies, and what I can't figure out is, what if I'm watching a movie from the '40s, you know, before widescreen. Like, say I'm watching *White Heat*. Is that '40s or '50s? Anyway, it's not widescreen. Would Cagney's face be stretched out in a grotesque fashion, beyond recognition? When I close my eyes I can imagine how Jimmy Cagney's big, wide, stretched-out face would look, taking up the whole screen. It's nightmarish. There's probably a button you can push to fix the aspect ratio, don't you think?"

"Our TV is fine," said the nature poet.

"Well, if I take custody of our TV, what are you going to do for TV?"

"I'm not big on TV."

"I've seen you watch a lot of TV. I've seen you watch the worst stuff. Lifetime movies. A young teacher goes on vacation and some unsavory fellows videotape her on the beach then edit the results to make her look sleazy and sell it on the internet. Her professional and personal lives suffer as a result. The wedding is called off. She fights to regain her dignity."

"*Caught on Tape*," said the nature poet. "I forget the subtitle."

"Those Lifetime movies always have subtitles. I love it!"

"I think I can live without it. I've enjoyed not having it around."

"What, are you going to be one of those people who goes around saying, 'I don't even own a TV'?"

"Maybe."

"It's like I don't even know you," said Cookie.

They laughed. It was one of their standard lines. But they stopped laughing sooner than usual. Then they changed the subject to why she had started buying unscented antiperspirant for them. Cookie could never remember whether or not he had put it on.

Cookie did eventually make the long drive to the big city to pick up the TV. He wasn't sure which dramatic event he thought would happen, but whatever it was, it didn't.

He and his wife walked across the street that night to a tapas restaurant with a huge picture window and the business of the city going on outside. They ordered a number of exotic dishes, like mashed green plantains with pork cracklings and an aromatic broth and tiny shrimp. It all came mixed together in a shallow silver bowl with a silver lid, and when they opened the lid up came the aromatic steam from the aromatic broth.

Cookie was going to miss stuff like that: aromatic broth and stuff.

They slept in the same bed that night. It was friendly. The bedroom had a lot of books in it.

"What about your books?" said Cookie's wife.

"I don't care about them anymore," said Cookie. "I know each one of them even in the dark, just by the vague sight of their spines. I see a pale one, which is *Journal of a West India Proprietor*. I remember where I bought it. City Lights in San Francisco. In 1999! The last century. I never read it. Last time I opened it, the pages were brown. I keep meaning to read it. Now I know I never will, and part of me is relieved. All of me."

The nature poet laughed.

"What?"

"I'm giving up TV and you're giving up books," she said.

They both laughed. They laughed and laughed.

Ha ha ha. It was so friendly.

The next morning, when the big, ugly TV had been lugged out of the penthouse and wedged into the small car, Cookie knew he was really going to leave. It was too hard to imagine hauling it back up.

The slogan on the license plate had taken on a melancholy resonance.

They kissed goodbye in the parking garage, among the rancid perfumes.

Cookie kept in touch with his wife, calling her, for example, the time he found a lump on his wrist.

"It's probably a ganglion," she said.

"You know everything," he said.

"They used to call them Bible bumps," she said.

"Bible bumps!" he said.

"They'd smash the ganglion with something big and heavy, like the old family Bible. The fluid would disperse and go back where it's supposed to go."

6

Now that he and his wife were living apart, Cookie often found himself reminiscing about the jerk who had refused to let her bum a smoke. True, his wife was a champion mooch.

He remembered how they saw the town cobbler leaning on a lamppost with his ciggie and a certain look on his face like a horrible movie star.

"Hey," said the nature poet, "can I be really bad and ask you for one of those?"

"No," said the cobbler.

Everybody laughed. The cobbler had the short, bitter laugh of a character whose stage directions said, *He gives a short, bitter laugh.*

"You can have a drag of this one."

The cobbler held out threateningly, in the nature of a challenge, the soggy, crimped end.

"That's okay," said the nature poet.

Cookie and the nature poet walked home.

The town square was a mile away from their quarters over the dentist's office in the strip mall and the walk required confronting some desolation under the stars, but usually they enjoyed the exercise.

Tonight they walked fast and felt agitated and insulted. Their hands wanted something to do. They had to shake the energy out through their hands.

"Wow," said Cookie.

"I know," said the nature poet.

"What was that about?" said Cookie.

"I guess I learned my lesson."

"I guess you'll never do that again."

"I guess not."

That night Cookie lay in bed and thought about taking the cigarette out of the cobbler's hand and poking the red end into the cobbler's cheekbone.

Just two days later he heard that the cobbler had been hospitalized with an intestinal parasite that nearly killed him.

A grudge was a petty shame. The cobbler had many good qualities and practiced the noble old trade of his forebears. He did not deserve to be struck down by an intestinal parasite, leaving behind a precious little son and grieving widow just because he had refused to fork over a cigarette to the woman Cookie loved.

Now the woman he loved had gone back to the big city, and why did Cookie think about that cigarette so much?

He should have taken better care of his wife. Was that proprietary and old-fashioned? Was it sexist? He wished he had been a better husband. It was like prodding at a wound, thinking of a world in which people could be dismissive toward her, try to put her in her place. She had a place all right. It was a great place, miles up in the air. Everybody else could suck it.

Pinkeye

I was strolling toward the high school on the opening day of football season when I saw a five-dollar bill fly out of the pocket of a little girl's shorts. By the time I scooped it up, she had gamboled quite a distance down the block. I wanted to run up to her and say, "Little girl, you dropped this." But then I pictured myself, a stout and ugly man of the town, a bachelor past my prime, wheezing as I dangled a five-dollar bill in the face of an unattended child in the town square on this busiest of days. Though I had no reason to be ashamed, the picture was too unseemly to contemplate. I put the money in my pocket and kept walking.

The little girl rushed forward to meet a group of friends, other little girls. Something else flew from her pocket, a single this time. I kept that too.

Now the girl had stopped. She and her knot of chattering playmates were concerned about something. They scowled and carried on, hands on hips in a miniature attitude of high drama that was quite charming, though my heart was chilled with fear that one of them had seen me picking up the bills from the sidewalk. I passed them without incident, however, and continued toward campus. On the way, I stopped at the Chevron station and bought a pack of cigarettes with a portion of my loot.

We have no opera house. Tailgating passes for art here. My friend's mother always puts out a tempting spread. I wolfed down pimento cheese sandwiches with the crusts cut off, homemade fried chicken, sugary ham biscuits, and other finger foods. I drank gin from an enormous cup and worked on a sunburn. Nothing could have been lovelier.

Four or five nephews (not my own) sported about in the grass with their toy football, waiting for the game to begin. I popped a whole slippery deviled egg into my mouth in order to take the hand of an old woman I did not recognize. She mentioned that her granddaughter had just been accepted into the Edinburgh Fringe Festival. I remarked in turn that the event was world famous, and she seemed surprised and delighted by the news.

"World famous!" she repeated. I did not trouble her with the fact that its true name is the Edinburgh Festival Fringe. Her garbling of the phrase is all too sadly common, even among the intelligentsia to whom I have been exposed in cyberspace.

It is a fact that I am more informed about entertainment and culture than many of my neighbors.

Something important had almost dawned on me the night before as I watched a crummy old movie about a French viscount escaping from a British prison.

The woman he loved helped get him across the channel, disguising herself as a shepherd and then as his "postboy."

There was the snooty Englishman—in love with the same woman—tracking him down.

There was his decadent French cousin who was happy the viscount had been put into prison. He was weak and foppish and awash in debt. He coveted the fortune that belonged rightfully to the viscount, and was so spineless he was willing to poison his old benefactor to get it quick.

There were various supporting players, such as the girl's feisty old aunt and an unshaven, double-crossing innkeeper.

It was awful.

The girl wore a tri-cornered hat and snug livery as she said, "Not now! Who has ever imagined a viscount kissing his postboy?"

"Everybody," I ventured aloud.

I thought it the kind of witticism that would go over big at a sophisticated party where everyone drank cocktails and poked fun at an old movie, just one sort of event for which this area is not primarily known.

It was late. I kept thinking I would turn off the TV and go to bed. But I could not deny that I wanted to see the snooty Englishman bested and the decadent fop get what was coming to him.

I wanted to see the girl—the worst actress in the world—glowing with connubial happiness.

I had trouble sleeping. Something was flitting there, not merely the girl in her tight boy suit. The next day, amidst the bright revelry, I tried to grasp it still.

One of the little nephews of my friend bumped into my legs, distracted by squinting at the instructions on a medicine bottle with a pink cap. He neither begged my pardon nor acknowledged my existence.

"What's wrong with that child?" I asked my friend. "Is he sick?"

"Pinkeye," answered the old woman, who had overheard.

"So I should completely avoid him?" my burly friend asked in a jocular tone of voice. He is large and full of life and enjoys joshing about his supposed vulnerability to the vagaries of fate.

"I don't worry about germs anymore," said the old woman, whose hand I had clasped so warmly. What a luxury, I thought, to be an old woman who no longer cares about germs.

In a coffee shop I had witnessed a little boy ineffectually stifling his liquid cough in the crook of his arm as he stood over one container full of straws and another full of spoons. Nearby, his brother, smaller still, spun the postcard rack around and around with something like viciousness. Nonetheless, I took no pleasure in the cruelty of the marketing executive who had decided to put pinkeye medicine in a little white bottle with a bright pink cap.

"Children remind me of that once-famous achondroplastic fellow now in the shameful regional commercial," I told my friend. "Have you seen it? He is forced to say, 'I'm short on cash.' I never cared for him at the height of his popularity, yet I am moved when I consider what he goes through. Ha ha, 'height of popularity,' that's marvelous, his unusually short stature being the sole source of his notoriety."

"Jen and I are going to have a baby," my friend said.

"Have I ever told you about the couple my brother knew who had a pet chimpanzee with cancer?" I replied. "This was in New Orleans, the Crescent City. For a long time you could walk by their house and see the chimpanzee glaring out the window at you. It was very sick. The husband was a wine merchant. He traveled around the nation to fabulous restaurants and sometimes he would take his wife along. During one of these professional visits, a rather famous chef in Charleston asked where the wife was and the fellow answered very matter-of-factly, 'She couldn't come. She's taking the chimpanzee for chemotherapy.' The chef made a certain face, so my brother's friend smashed a valuable champagne flute in his eyes. The traveling wine salesman felt insulted and judged. Perhaps he was sensitive. You may be asking yourself, 'What were the consequences of his rash actions?'"

But my friend had ceased to listen to me. He was huddled together with his tiny wife, with whom he seemed to be sharing a private joke. I examined her figure for signs of pregnancy and saw none.

I have nothing against babies per se. People are fascinated by their own babies, perhaps with good reason.

A typical conversation with a parent might go something like this:

"After Maddy's nap, I either heat a bottle of breast milk or mix up a bottle of formula. Marcie pumps at work and puts the milk in these little plastic bags for me to use at home. We've been feeding her baby food for about the last month, too. She likes sweet potatoes."

"Hmm."

"Avocado."

"Exotic and promising!"

"Squash."

"That's good."

"Green beans."

"An old classic!" (Here, his gracious avocado sentiment having been ignored, the secondary participant is trying again to muster some excitement and bring the discussion around to something more universal.)

"Green peas."

"Those I'm not so crazy about. But I'm sure they're good for a baby." (Introducing a Hegelian dynamic to jazz things up.)

"Beef baby food."

"My, what a hungry baby."

"After you feed Maddy, you need to burp her. I either set her on my knee or put her on my shoulder and pat her back. It's fun when you get a big burp. It's funny when a big burp comes out of that little mouth. Sometimes you can hear the air coming up her throat right before it comes out of her mouth. Sometimes Maddy spits up. It's mostly pretty random. You just wipe it up. Once or twice I've changed shirts when she spit up on my shoulder. And about once I've changed her outfit because it was so wet from spit-up. She seemed to amuse herself a few months ago by waiting for me to change a soiled diaper, then going again as we were putting the new diaper on. Sometimes she would do it two or three times in a row. I hope that means she's going to have a funny sense of humor. I've heard her laugh repeatedly twice. I mean, not just a random laugh, but a prolonged bout of laughter that had some object to it."

Once I suffered through just such a conversation with a former friend, a man called Mr. Harris. He was rather aged for a new father, which may have accounted for the otherwise unaccountable relish with which he employed such coprolalia.

"Why is it," I asked him, getting into the spirit of things, "that a cat knows not to crap on the floor from the very day of its birth, but a baby will gladly crap in its own pants without a second thought?"

"But then a baby learns to talk," said Mr. Harris. "What does a cat learn?"

"One of Little Jimmy Parker's twins crapped on my break-fast table when she was a baby," I informed him. "The other one crapped in my new porch swing. I think you could give babies a serum. Something with feline genomes in it or something. I just had an idea for a product. Something you put in a cat's diet so its feces smell good."

"Lavender," said Mr. Harris.

"Really?"

"I don't know," said Mr. Harris. "It might work."

For a moment it was there, the familiar spark. Mr. Harris was my old science teacher, and how we had always loved to come up with ideas for products. None of them amounted to anything, but our dreams kept us going. After he married his much younger wife—a former biology lab partner of mine, in fact—nothing was ever the same.

I observed the long table of tailgating dainties, so lately full of promise, all of which the infected nephew had rummaged through with antic physicality. Hands in pockets, I took my leave.

I smoked as I walked, recalling, as I often did, a father who was carrying his baby around a department store. The child was not wearing shoes, a fact I noted aloud at the time, as the temperature outside had taken an unseasonable and precipitous dip. I thought perhaps that the father had been shopping in the department store for some hours and was unaware of the change in weather.

"You know who says things like that?" the father responded. "Old ladies."

He said it in a jesting and harmless fashion, as we had known one another for some years. I went on to humorously respond, "That is exactly what I am!" The humor derived from the fact that I am middle-aged and male. I was poking fun at my own shortcomings to be a good sport.

The father went on to describe how an actual "old lady" had come up to his wife, who was carrying their boy in her arms at the time. The old lady in question grabbed the baby's bare foot and remarked, "His feet are like ice!"

The wife jerked her baby away from the old lady's grasp and said, "Don't you dare touch my baby."

This story was presented as an example of bravery and fortitude on the part of the wife. The teller's face shone with pride as he related the manner in which his wife had snarled at an old lady. I could not help feeling somewhat chastened, albeit it in a passive and not unpleasant way. At the same time I was bewildered.

Similarly, my thoughts were crazed and muddy as I walked home from the football game, a state of mind I welcomed. Hot air balloons, the electric coffee pot, the poetry of William Blake—here are just a few of the items we would not be able to enjoy today if someone had pushed a crazy thought to the back of his head because he didn't want to brood about it.

The Bible says something about a "still, small voice." What a beautiful thought. Another Biblical phrase is "like a thief in the night." Inspiration does not come crashing and stumbling like a lout.

Few of us are old enough to remember homemade crystal radio sets, a pastime of yore. I do not believe I ever put one together successfully, yet somehow I retain a mental image of the process, possibly from a movie. What I am picturing is the infinite patience with which the young enthusiast groped for a signal. Somewhere, from the stars, a message!

I would not have to get my teeth fixed to become a so-called "Hollywood character actor," portraying the henchman or goon of a corrupt and oleaginous Southern senator, saying things like, "Get in the car." My unfortunate smile might even turn out to be a benefit.

"He's authentic! He's the real thing!" Such encomia I could imagine bursting from the lips of agents and casting directors as I stood by modestly within earshot.

Upon arriving home, I made up a list of the good points and bad points about my town.

Good: friends.

Bad: a chemical smell.

Good: plans to revitalize the economy through tourism.

Bad: tourism based on an infamous murder in a creepy doll hospital.

Good: flowers.

Bad: a dog somewhere that barks all night.

Good: old-fashioned hobby shop provides nostalgia and irony in equal measures.

Bad: racists.

The list thus completed, I called my friend. It was halftime, and the marching band was playing.

"There is nothing keeping me here anymore," I said. "I'm off to pursue my dreams."

My friend said, "Who is this?" He said, "Hello?"

Joan Crawford:
A Hot-Looking Woman

ROBERT MONTGOMERY DUMPED JOAN CRAWFORD AT THE ALTAR.
After that, there was a jump cut to Joan Crawford chopping wood at
a mountain cabin.

"There she is, chopping wood!" I said aloud.

My girlfriend would have known what I meant, but she didn't
come over anymore.

Maybe I was drunk, but Joan Crawford was a hot-looking woman. I could watch her chopping wood all day long. It wasn't her fault
people turned her into a camp figure later on. Time turns us all into
camp figures in the end.

Jerry Lewis

AN OPEN BOX OF DOUGHNUTS ON THE COFFEE TABLE. LITTLE BULLETS lined up in a pretty little row. The girl working on the chamber of a revolver with a little tool like a Q-tip expressly designed for the purpose. Her yellow hair hanging in her eyes.

Girl with a half-fastened holster, like a male gangster in a movie.

Girl in a sleeveless corrugated T, low scooped neck, like a male gangster in a movie.

Girl in striped boxers, like a male gangster in a movie.

She looked up.

Humphries jerked back his head, away from the dirty window into which he had accidentally peeped.

What was he supposed to do now? Something?

She opened the door.

"Hi," said Humphries. "I'm looking for a cat."

His eyes went to the empty holster.

"Are you a policeman?" he blurted.

"What gave me away, the doughnuts?"

"What doughnuts?"

She laughed like a sexy crow. The way she talked was also like a sexy crow, one of those crows that can talk. But sexy. Her teeth were so white they were almost blue. They looked like happy ghosts. She said, "Have you ever seen the movie *Hardly Working*?"

"I don't think so. What's it about?"

"Jerry Lewis is on a job interview at the post office. He's really hungry. He hasn't eaten for days. So while the guy's trying to interview him, all he can see is this box of doughnuts on the desk. He's not listening at all. The guy finally asks him, 'Do you want a doughnut?' And Jerry goes, 'Where ARE DEY?' Just like that. 'Where ARE DEY?'"

She laughed some more.

Humphries made himself laugh. He was nervous because where was the gun? In the dewy small of her back, tucked in the waistband of her boxers? He had seen something like that in a movie.

"I'm not a cop," said the woman.

"My wife's cat is missing," said Humphries. "He's orange? Sometimes I see a black cat on this porch, sitting on this thing." Humphries pointed to the rusted glider, its filthy vinyl cushions illustrated—defiled—with big blotchy flowers. "I don't know, I felt my wife's cat might have sought out the company of another cat? He's not used to being outside and she's very worried, understandably. We recently moved here to Mississippi from Vermont, which is generally considered a more civilized state, no offense, and my wife is understandably concerned that there might be some barefoot children who have reverted to some kind of savagery and walk around trying to shoot little cats with a bow and arrow."

"I'm from Chicago, dude. I don't give a shit. Want to know what I would have told you if you hadn't seen the gun? My cover story is that I'm looking for a place to live out in the sticks because I want to have a baby. I'm thirty-nine. If I wait any longer, there's some danger involved for the baby. I mean, there's a pretty good chance of something going wrong chromosomally, am I right? Where am I going to bring up the baby I want to have? Chicago? All the neighborhoods are getting too expensive, even the bad neighborhoods. There was a torso on a mattress. Where we lived. In the alley below our apartment. They found a headless torso on a mattress. And the place was still too expensive for us. Is that where I'm going to raise a kid? Like, 'Look out the window, there's a torso on a mattress.' Like, 'Mommy, what's a torso?' And we can't even afford *that*. Like, 'Sorry, lady, the torso on the mattress is extra.' Jocko had some prospects down here—my cover-story husband who doesn't actually exist, that's Jocko—so here we are, anyway. He wants to do voiceovers. He wants to be a voiceover guy, my made-up husband does. He can do that from anywhere. He just needs a good microphone and a special phone line."

Humphries couldn't believe she was thirty-nine. She looked like a girl, like a college kid or something. Like an inspirational young teacher fresh from the academy with a lot of exciting notions about how to change the world. She had a gun.

"Come on in," she said.

"I really need to keep looking."

"Could be I have some information about your cat. Sorry. Your *wife's* cat." She said it like she didn't believe he had a wife.

"Really?"

She shrugged.

Humphries was scared but titillated. He followed her inside.

The place was dank. It smelled the way other people's places always do: like the long-unwashed pillowcase of a much-sought-after courtesan—sour milk and violets.

"What'll it be?"

"Ovaltine?" said Humphries.

She turned from him without humor and headed for the kitchen, scratching her ass in an elegant way.

Humphries sat on the couch where he had seen her sitting. The bullets and pistol were magically gone. The doughnuts remained.

There were two flies walking on the doughnuts. He thought the seat cushion felt warm from her, or maybe everything was warm.

Who was she? Why did she need a cover story? Obviously she knew nothing about Mr. Mugglewump. Chicago was where hitmen came from. Something awful was going to happen and Humphries would never be seen again. Part of him thought that would be okay.

She came back with a couple of Rolling Rocks. She handed one to Humphries. It was fairly warm, like everything else.

She sat cattycorner to Humphries, on an armchair that looked to be upholstered in some sort of immensely uncomfortable material, like tweed. It would make little red marks on the backs of her bare legs, he thought. Fascinating crosshatched patterns.

"This place is a hole," she said.

She twisted the switch on a shabby lamp. It seemed to have a brown bulb. At least it leaked a brownish light that made things darker.

"Please, Officer, I'll tell you whatever you want to know," joked Humphries. He shielded his eyes as if from the bare bulb of a searing interrogation.

She didn't get it.

When Humphries and his wife were trying to find a place, they had attended an open house for which the realtor had decorated the gates with brown balloons in welcome. Brown balloons! It was an odd choice. It was odd that expensive factory machinery would be put into place to manufacture brown balloons.

"Stay right there," she said. "If you ever want to see Fluffy again, ha ha." She got up and went back to the kitchen. For cigarettes, Humphries assumed somehow. His hands were sweating. There were sexual feelings mingled with terror. He got up and ran out the door, knocking over a small table, clattering.

He ran down the street. He hadn't run anywhere since boyhood.

Thank goodness Mr. Mugglewump came home that night.

"Where have you *been*?" Humphries cooed over him, and so did Humphries's wife Mrs. Josie Humphries.

The cat couldn't tell where he had been.

Neither could Humphries.

Now I have a terrible secret, he thought.

He lay in bed next to Josie and had private visions of torment.

It was a small neighborhood. He would run into the mysterious siren. Maybe Josie, who loved a pleasant stroll, would be on his arm when the confrontation occurred! All scenarios were distasteful.

He couldn't sleep.

Humphries read the *New York Times* on the internet every day like a big shot. He disdained the local rag. It was a way to get back at his wife, who had moved to this Podunk burg for a job. Humphries was a landscape painter, so he could live anywhere. That's what Josie said. But what was he supposed to paint around here? A ditch? He stood on the back porch every day and painted pictures of turds for spite. Josie said they were good.

She was all right.

She noticed that Humphries started walking down to the drugstore in the morning and picking up the local paper. She made knowing faces at him. Now that Mr. Mugglewump had survived on the streets, Mississippi was looking okay to her. Humphries cringed and shuddered at her implicit optimism and got back to the paper. He was looking for a story about some local jerk getting assassinated.

On the third day he almost gave up because he didn't want to give his wife the satisfaction. But he rose in the first smeary light, while Josie was still asleep, and walked to the drugstore. He didn't have to bring the paper home. Without that clue, Josie wouldn't be able to guess he was happy. Because he was happy. He was happy being miserable. He was happy that living in Mississippi would give him a great excuse to be a failure.

There were some old codgers spitting in a cup for some reason. Humphries stood on the corner reading about Buddy Wilson, who had owned a struggling poster shop. He was a large fat man who had been found at the county dump, his head nearly severed from his body. Police suspected garroting by banjo string because there was a banjo lying nearby with a missing string.

It was cool out. Humphries's palms were sweating. He threw the paper in a trashcan and wiped the slippery newsprint on his pants. For the first time, he went back to the house where he had spotted the girl with the gun.

The window glowed. He could see everything from the street. It was like a different place, draped in fabrics, oranges and pinks, full of light and life. The homey smell of bacon was in the air.

A young couple—nothing like the yellow-haired girl with the gun—pulled a twee red sweater over their little white dog. They had a string of white Christmas lights blinking along the mantle, though Christmas was miles and miles away.

The dirty old glider was still on the porch. It was the only thing to convince Humphries he wasn't crazy.

He had a bad day and couldn't get any turds painted.

That evening, just before the sun went down, he went back to the odd little duplex. The young couple had put up curtains. The black cat, a fixture of the neighborhood, was back in its place on the soiled glider. The white dog in the red sweater stood smugly on its hind legs between the curtain and the window with its white forepaws on the window ledge, safely behind the glass, staring at the cat with sick superiority.

Cancel My Reservation

1

ON HIS WALK, CHUCK PASSED A CHURCH. HE SAW SOME BIRDS. He didn't know what kind. They were brown, pecking at something—what do birds peck at? seeds?—on the lawn. He caught himself thinking, They have their mouths open! Indeed, when the birds turned to him with their frozen faces, not eating but not closing their mouths, they looked dumbstruck and evil. But birds have beaks, not mouths. Upon reflection.

He was not good with details. He had even become fat without knowing it. Thinking back, he really couldn't imagine not noticing that his clothes were so tight, not wondering why he had to wear his shirts untucked and unbutton his pants, why he didn't wear a belt anymore and his knees hurt so much, why it was hard to rise from a crouch and how come he had so much trouble breathing and broke the toilet seat.

He didn't know the right name or purpose of anything in nature. He saw a bank of flowers, the kind he wrongly called coolers—grape coolers, cherry coolers, vanilla coolers—bright and cheap as candy, trash flowers, pretty as paper stars or costume jewelry, the kind of flowers you might find planted in black plastic drums near the gas pumps. He saw an embankment of them ashen, crumpled, bubble-gum colors chewed up, sucked out, and discarded by the heat.

His scratchy shirt was long-sleeved and hot. It was early in the morning and already miserable in the sun. Saints used to wear scratchy shirts—hairshirts, right? It was good for you. It made you stop concentrating on your thoughts and opinions, that was probably the gist of it.

He kept walking to the old graveyard.

Used to be you couldn't go in: too many bums waiting to cut your throat. So said the pro-gentrification forces on local talk radio. Now it was safe to look at the old headstones. They were good for a laugh.

Leak. Hope. Luckie. Shedden. He thought those were pretty funny names to see on tombstones. He planned to jot them down on a pad when he got home. Later he'd show it to somebody for a conversation piece. He was sad to have lost touch with Donny. Donny loved wordplay.

He saw a tombstone that said Stocks. That was only funny depending on the stock market.

Not everything was funny. He saw a black log, dead or burnt, part of a tree that had come through the ground, come out of somebody's head and knocked aside his granite lozenge. He saw four stubby matching stones in a little parade. Their squat bases said: Mama. Papa. Honey. Me.

One squirrel grabbed a twig from a clump of plants with purple leaves, took the purple leafy twig to the top of a grave to chew.

Angry squirrels romping. Owned the place. Probably had it to themselves for fifty years or something, except for the bums. He guessed the squirrels weren't so tough anymore. Too bad, you squirrels and bums. The rich people are taking over.

The walk helped him think. Chuck went home and got really drunk and booked a first-class round-trip airplane ticket from Atlanta to LAX and back. It cost nearly a thousand. For sixty bucks more he could've upgraded to a plan that allowed him to change his flight or cancel his trip, but however drunk he was he wasn't that drunk. Not hardly.

2

Donny and Chuck had reconnected on Facebook. At first it was okay with Donny. Chuck made a friend request and Donny complied. He didn't see why not. Chuck showered him with private chat messages right away.

Hi, it's Chuck. Remember me Donny
hey man long time hows it been goin
My wife passed away.
did not know you were married congrats
Yes, but she passed away.
sorry
Hey aren't we lucky we turned out to be the wrong age to be in any wars? At least we got that going for us, haha

That was sad about Chuck's wife passing away. Donny found out that Chuck had had two wives, and both of them had passed away, which was twice as sad. Maybe it was exponentially sad. Donny couldn't believe Chuck had married hot-to-trot Shelly Riviera straight out of high school. Donny had moved out of the district halfway through his junior year, but he still remembered the name Shelly Riviera. He wasn't sure if he was putting the right face and body with the name. He was thinking of some hot girl he had permanently in his head.

Chuck had an estranged son. Donny found out everything about Chuck. His favorite canned soup. Chuck told stories about his two wives and how sexy they had been when they were alive and all their sex things.

Sometimes Donny got hard and secretly beat off, Chuck none the wiser. Or maybe Chuck was egging him on. Who was in charge here?

Soon he didn't want to see Chuck around Facebook anymore. He was so tired of Chuck and Chuck's crazy stories and opinions. He was scared of how much he was beating off these days. He was too old for such horseshit. He told Chuck he had a fatal disease and couldn't chat anymore.

Chuck's private messages became devastated. He wanted to know whether it was cancer.

no its none of the big ones you never heard of it

Donny realized that the only way to make the story stick was to leave Facebook altogether. He deleted his account and it was a great relief. He found that he didn't miss Facebook at all.

The only thing that concerned him was his lie about dying. Donny couldn't recall any specific examples, but he had a strong feeling that he had lied a couple of times before and the lie had always come true. Had he maybe lied about being poked in the eye with a stick? And then had something happened to his eye at the beach? Or was that somebody else?

3

It was Chuck's first time in first class.

A woman behind him was talking loudly about a person who was a "dick."

Across the aisle a man referred to the spare tire around his middle as "this fucking thing."

They should call it First Crass, ha ha, thought Chuck.

But seriously, why were people so crass?

He didn't care too much because of all the pills he had taken. He could stretch out his legs while the nice people brought him drinks.

He looked down at his loafers and remembered how his second wife had always made him wear shoes with laces. He said, "I was never any good at tying my shoes," and she said, "I wouldn't go around admitting that either." And he said, "What do you mean *either?*" And she laughed and said, "I don't know."

Chuck laughed too. They laughed a lot. Veda didn't want kids. Neither did Chuck. He already had one, and look how that turned out. It was a racket. But he brooded about what she said: "I wouldn't go around admitting that either." Freudian! What was the other thing? There was some other thing about Chuck that shamed Veda, something she never told him, something she nursed deep inside.

Then she got the terrible virus that improved their relationship but weakened and killed her. She left him a good bit of money and a big life insurance policy, about which he hadn't known. He cashed her substantial retirement account and his too when he quit his job. He had not expected to live very long without her.

The money was running out, but he kept spending it however suited him. Most of the time he couldn't think of anything, which was why it had lasted.

They gave him a good hot breakfast in first class, with a real fork and knife. They gave him his choice of cookies.

Chuck drank and took pills and lived all the time in a fog that wasn't too bad. He had mostly crushed down his emotions. He hadn't had a normal thought in two solid years. But these new pills the doctor had given him for the airplane didn't work. The plane seemed to slow down at weird times in the middle of the air.

Chuck was scared.

———

4

Chuck's knowledge of Hollywood geography was based on snippets of things he had heard on television. He ended up way out in Burbank, a fifty-dollar cab ride from Beverly Hills, where he had business.

But he liked the hotel. His stay was going to cost him a thousand, but what the hell. Seemed like everything about California cost a thousand. He had a thousand to spend on his official business, too.

Chuck liked that there was a drugstore across the street. There were lots of things across the street. It was a good location. You could go across the street and get anything, even a cat from the pet store. Chuck traveled light, and he liked the easy access to necessities. His terror of airplanes had kept him out of the air for a while. He knew about the latest measures—that he would have to take off his shoes and belt, for example. He practiced taking off his shoes and belt at home and got really good at it. But he didn't want to be held up in security by some zealot who thought his bottle of shampoo was explosive or his phone might trigger a bomb. So he didn't bring a phone. Why would he need one? People just thought they needed stuff. Chuck had seen a commercial where a guy bragged about his Kindle being like "a thousand books in your back pocket." Only a moron or an unimaginably perverse monomaniac would need a thousand books in his back pocket. A thousand books in your back pocket was not a good thing. One book at a time in your back pocket was plenty. Zero was also good. Hotels supplied free shampoo, soap, shower gel. They would give you a toothbrush and toothpaste if you asked. Anything else he needed, Chuck could get at the drugstore.

Chuck was hungry for dinner at three thirty in the afternoon because of the time difference. He went to the "bistro" across the street. It was empty that time of day, but open. Chuck ordered roasted chicken and French fries. He sat at the bar, a black cloth napkin on his lap. A guy in a burgundy apron waited on him. A guy with a Russian accent popped up from the back and made genial, lewd comments about life. Chuck ordered some rosé and the Russian complimented him on his selection then loudly cursed the man in the apron, who had disappeared. The man in the apron came back. A third guy showed up. Everybody stood around doing nothing.

His first wife Shelly had worked in restaurants, and Chuck knew it was unusual for people who worked in a restaurant to stand around doing nothing. Wasn't there silverware to roll? The Russian guy told the other two he would get dinner for them. He got on the phone and loudly, almost abrasively, ordered a pizza and two chicken parms from some Italian place. Chuck thought that was interesting, but who cared? His roasted chicken was good when it came out. It looked like a picture. When the third guy carried it over to him, he stopped on the way and showed it to the man in the apron, like it was something special. Was that a sincere move or showmanship? It was like neither of them had ever seen a chicken before. Had no one ever ordered the chicken before? They seemed so amazed. Chuck was in a blur from the airplane booze and airplane pills and regular booze and regular pills. He dug in, breaking through the gorgeous, shiny skin.

Back at the hotel, Chuck used his key card to get into the "Business Center." It was some closet with a tiny wastebasket and a computer. Chuck guessed that business centers had atrophied since the last time he had been in one. Everybody was his or her own business center now.

Chuck signed into Twitter and announced to his followers that he was in L.A. He'd sure love someone to show him the ropes.

He was surprised to get a direct message right away with a phone number from Maria Garey, whom he didn't remember following or being followed by.

He called her from his room. Probably nobody used in-room telephones anymore. The hotel was going to love Chuck so much. He felt happy to make them happy. He felt like maybe they would give him special treatment because he was such a big spender.

Chuck and Maria caught up a bit, exclaiming how great it was to hear each other's voices, how they couldn't believe each other remembered each other, how of course they remembered each other, are you kidding? Maria remembered that Chuck had married Shelly Riviera. Chuck had to tell her Shelly was dead. Maria was so sorry. Chuck said it was okay. It happened a long time ago, when they were young. It was sad that Shelly had died young, but they had been having difficulties. She died in a small plane crash, taking flying lessons from her clandestine lover. There had been a lot of anger mixed up with the grief. Chuck was too young to be a husband and he was a terrible father, but being so young and resilient and selfish at the time had helped him heal. Maria said that was great, all that stuff about the healing and everything.

"Their skeletons were mingled," said Chuck.

"Oh no!" said Maria.

"So you live out here?" said Chuck.

"I'm just off Beverly Glen."

"Is that near Beverly Hills?" said Chuck. "I have to be in Beverly Hills tomorrow."

"As a matter of fact, it is."

"Well, they both have 'Beverly' in the name," said Chuck.

"What are you doing out here?" said Maria.

"Do you remember Donny Billings?"

"I don't think so."

"Oh, well, he left in eleventh grade, was it? He had big ears and freckles."

"I just don't know."

"Brillo pad hair?"

Maria made a noise like she didn't remember.

"Dark red, but like a Brillo pad. They called him Brillo Head. Do you remember the guy, Brillo Head, they said he tried to choke himself with his mother's bra?"

"You'd think I'd remember something like that," said Maria.

"That's Donny, anyway. He's real sick now."

"I'm sorry to hear it," said Maria.

"Yeah, he's, uh, they don't think he's going to make it. I was going to send him a 'get well' thing, and I remember he always liked Bob Hope. So I was going to send him this, like, Bob Hope thing."

"That's cool," said Maria.

"Yeah, so they're doing this auction of Bob Hope's personal effects."

"I want to go!" said Maria.

"Do you really?"

"It sounds cool."

"It's tomorrow afternoon."

"I can't do tomorrow afternoon."

"That's too bad," said Chuck. "Well, it's on Saturday, too."

"Saturday might happen," said Maria. "Let me check into it. I'm having some people for dinner Friday night, tomorrow night. You should definitely come. What time is your auction over?"

"I don't know, I've never been to one."

"Well, here, let me give you my address."

She gave him her address.

"Just come over when it's done, or call me or whatever. I'm making red beans and rice. It's kind of loose."

"So what are you doing out here?" said Chuck.

"This is embarrassing, but I'm a writer on a TV show," said Maria.

"Why is that embarrassing?" said Chuck.

"It's not," said Maria.

"What show?" said Chuck.

"*Elevated Feelings*," said Maria.

"I don't know that one."

"It has a cult following. It's quite popular, actually. The *New York Times* called it one of the top twelve programs of the year three years ago."

"Is it on one of those pay stations?"

"Oh, no, it's just basic cable."

"I liked it better when there were just three channels."

"That was a long time ago," said Maria.

"Yes," said Chuck. He was falling asleep.

"I'm glad there are more channels, or I'd be out of a job."

5

It must have been 1979 or '80, because Donny hadn't moved yet. There were three channels on TV. Chuck always liked to talk about how much better things had been when there were just three channels on TV. A kid was forced to grapple with cultural objects no kid today would ever discover. Kids today had too many choices, and as a result their worldview was paradoxically and oppressively narrow. They could watch *Finding Nemo* over and over. There were channels with nothing but cartoons. A kid in the 1970s would find himself watching Harold Lloyd on a Sunday afternoon—a silent, black-and-white movie! Unthinkable now.

All through the seventies Chuck had watched something called "The Big Show," an afternoon movie franchise on the local CBS affiliate. They were mostly black-and-white. The weatherman introduced them. There was one about a giant tarantula. A Tarzan movie came on most Fridays. Chuck remembered one with these two supple trees growing side by side. The natives would bend the trees toward one another and bind them. They tied some safari dude's legs to the trees, one to each tree. Then they cut the rope and the trees whanged away from one another. You just saw the tops of the trees flying in opposite directions but you heard the guy go *Eeeeeyaaaawwwww* and knew he had been ripped in half, down the middle, wishbone style. It was intense.

By the time Donny and Chuck were juniors, "The Big Show" had some competition on Channel Ten. It was this thing called "Movies 10," and it was too cool to have a host. There was just an animated opening graphic, some psychedelia on a cherry-red background of a guy with a movie camera disintegrating into cubist components. Then the movie would come on. Hipper stuff than "The Big Show" could get: *Harry and Walter Go to New York, The Hot Rock, Popi, Where's Poppa?, The Pink Panther, The Choirboys, Cotton Comes to Harlem, California Split, Super Fuzz, Freebie and the Bean, Uptown Saturday Night, Little Murders.* Heavily edited, most of them, but they made you feel you were getting away with something.

Donny was absent for a few weeks and everybody said he had tried to strangle himself with his mother's bra. Donny had no father and a strange mother from Germany. Once Chuck had gone over there for lunch and she made tuna salad with pineapple rings on it. They kept the house dark.

Homeroom signed a card for Donny. Chuck volunteered to take it over.

Donny opened the door and seemed glad to see him. The house smelled funny.

Donny invited Chuck in. He said *Cancel My Reservation* was just coming on "Movies 10."

Donny's mother and sister were gone, so Donny had the house to himself. Chuck thought that was odd. He was kind of nervous. Donny was apparently a maniac of some sort, though he appeared calm and peaceful. Chuck saw a full glass of Coke sitting on the carpet near the TV. The cola itself had a bluish slime growing on its flat, calm surface.

They watched *Cancel My Reservation* and Donny made a lot of insightful comments about Bob Hope's career. Chuck looked back on it as the first time he had ever heard anyone make insightful comments.

Chuck had never thought about Bob Hope one way or another. In those days, Bob Hope was just vaguely around, like the human appendix or lichens.

But Donny said things like, "Bob Hope and Eva Marie Saint are really good together. Can you believe she was with Marlon Brando in *On the Waterfront* and Cary Grant in *North by Northwest* and now here she is in this? You could argue that it places Bob Hope in the lineage of those titans, each representing a perfected but very different acting style. Or you might study Eva Marie Saint's talent for reacting. It's honest and true and puts her leading men in stark relief."

Later: "This is the most recent Bob Hope movie and it came out almost ten years ago. He's washed up in the movies. Can you believe this came out the same year Al Pacino revolutionized cinema acting forever in the Oscar-winning production of *The Godfather*?"

When the cameos by Flip Wilson and Johnny Carson came up, Donny laughed with wise appreciation and said, "This is commentary on Bob Hope's earlier movie career. A fitting elegy."

Chuck still remembered him saying that: "A fitting elegy." That's when he knew Donny was special, smarter than anybody else. Put it together with the attempted suicide via his mother's bra and you really had something in this Donny.

Plus, the things he said were true. Bob Hope and Eva Marie Saint *were* good together. They had a natural rhythm just like an old married couple. Chuck watched close after Donny said it, and he learned what marriage was that day, he really did.

Man oh man! That Donny.

Before one football game, Shelly Riviera had gone in the band room closet and let all the willing male band members feel her up, one at a time. The percussionists were first in line, followed by some of the cockier trumpeters who could hit the high notes. Girly instruments like woodwinds hung around on the fringe, not really knowing what was up. Chuck was third clarinet. He squeaked constantly. The first two clarinets were girls, which made Chuck a figure of some fun. This guy Damon who sat behind him used to take his lyre—a clamp for holding music during marching season—and attach it painfully to Chuck's earlobe, drawing blood. Damon once paid his own sister Tracy to sit on Chuck's lap and squirm lasciviously when the band bus broke down. She kept half-rising, pretending to look for something in the overhead compartment, and then she'd sit down and squirm some more. Damon and those guys were sitting in the back of the bus laughing. Chuck didn't get the joke. He thought it was the best night of his life until the band director broke it up. Damon was later electrocuted when trying to cut the wires on the band room clock.

It was Damon who maneuvered Chuck into line to feel up Shelly Riviera in the dark. She was wearing her band jacket and her frilled dickey with nothing underneath. Ominous tubas hung in dull cyclopean glints on the wall, waiting for concert season, when they would replace the cruder sousaphones.

Later Shelly told him he had been the politest boy to feel her up by far. He had been trying to channel the weary Bob of *Cancel My Reservation*.

A climactic scene of that movie involved the weaponizing of Eva Marie Saint's leopard-skin bra. Much business occurred with the bra. The bra was important to the plot. Characters examined it, pulled and fondled it, discussed and fretted over it. What an awful coincidence. Later Chuck realized that life is nothing but an awful coincidence. Without being too obvious, he kept an eye on Donny, who seemed to thoroughly relish the bra scene with no sign of troubled reflections. Whatever had been wrong with him, *Cancel My Reservation* made Donny feel better.

6

The back wall of the auction house was a dark, creamy orange on which Bob Hope's name was spelled out in sparkling golden paint with black accents.

Chuck was two hours early for the auction. Not many were so green. Only two of the folding chairs were occupied, to his surprise, by a heavy man in a neon pink Harley-Davidson T-shirt and a heavy woman wearing pajama pants and a surgical mask. For the first of many times, it was brought home to him with a thud that he was not Cary Grant in *North by Northwest*. He pegged a Christopher Hitchens lookalike with a parboiled face as serious competition, bent in mindful fury before the reception desk upon which his catalog was helplessly splayed. Even this man was dressed down, though his T-shirt was somber and advertised a highbrow museum exhibit.

Chuck had tried to dress up. He was in a blue velvet jacket with a loose string on the sleeve he couldn't stop looking at but was too afraid to pull.

Feeling self-conscious, Chuck headed straight for the back corner, where a horribly ugly Leroy Neiman painting hung in waiting.

Shelly had loved Leroy Neiman. She had also become obsessed with tanning later on. He never figured out Shelly.

Neiman's style made Chuck think of somebody weak trying to stab you to death.

Shelly liked this series Leroy Neiman had done for the Olympic Village, mostly showing athletes stretching and preening, but there was this one of a tiger crouched to spring with flashing eyes. "To fire them up," Shelly said. She had bought a cheap print of it and hung it over their bed. "For inspiration," she said.

The painting of Bob Hope was so godawful Chuck couldn't stop looking at it. Was that an oak tree? Why was it purple? Did golf courses usually have huge old oak trees standing right next to the tee? Chuck didn't know anything about golf. But where was that ball coming from, what physically impossible angle?

The worst was Bob Hope's face.

Bob's eyes had never been like that, so open and guileless. Neiman hadn't even managed to get the nose right, a feat any boardwalk caricaturist could have achieved. The most fearful impact was reserved for the mouth. This Hope wore the smile of an insane idiot. It felt like Neiman thought he was doing Hope a favor, smoothing him out, redacting his guarded smile and replacing it with something more palatable for public consumption. He had edited Hope, bowdlerized him. It was an insult. Bob was a cool customer, and Neiman couldn't understand it.

But it kept Chuck staring long enough that his outrage turned to something else. Maybe it was the fact that he had walked in just minutes ago and still felt fraudulent and out of his element. Maybe it was the pills. Chuck suddenly understood what Leroy Neiman was trying to get across: *This is how happy Bob Hope felt playing golf.* And it was all the more touching and humane for Neiman's incompetence. Insight married to incompetence! The consolations of art!

Bob had lived for a century, but now he was just as stone dead as Shelly Riviera or poor Veda or Kurt Cobain. Life's fleeting pleasures are the most important things, whispered the horrible Leroy Neiman painting of Bob Hope playing golf.

Chuck had left his catalog, for which he had paid one hundred dollars plus ten dollars shipping and handling, back in Atlanta. It was too bulky and awkward to carry on the plane. He found the real stuff in display cases lining the rooms of the auction house more compelling. Things he had flipped past on paper glowed at him now. He wanted to bust out Bob's "Studio Del Campo Enameled Copper Dishes" and lick their deep colors like candy.

He searched unsuccessfully for Bob Hope's ice bucket with the silver-plated polar bear on top. It was part of lot 21, the first thing he had marked down as a possible score—for himself or Donny, he couldn't decide. He knew what he *had* to get Donny: the dusty Native American pot, possibly imitation, set atop a modernistic, sickly bulging metal pedestal that shone like a mirror. The pot and pedestal didn't go together. Like Bob Hope and Eva Marie Saint! But they made it work by force. Chuck thought Donny would appreciate the tension. The pot had two handles that looked like squat, unsatisfied arms, hands on hips. It was a gruff dirt-colored pot with a lid like a frumpy hat. The plaque on the pedestal said, "From the Cast and Crew of CANCEL MY RESERVATION, 1971."

Everything had a plaque on it. Give Bob Hope an oversized pewter boot for his birthday, make damned sure to weld a plaque to it. Bob Hope had so much stuff he needed plaques to keep everything straight. What a life.

Another ice bucket, a cunning red apple with an incomprehensible brass plate screwed on: "TO BOB HOPE WITH BOUNDLESS THANKS FOR MAKING LIGHTS ON THE BENEFIT IN THE BIG APPLE." Making lights on the benefit? It had looked so nice in the catalog, ripe and polished plastic. In person it was a shabby apple, hardly able to support the mighty nonsense inscribed upon it.

Things that looked bad in the catalog looked good in real life, and vice versa. That was meaningful. Chuck had learned at least one important thing and there was still more than an hour to go before the auction started. He was never going to find that silver polar bear. It could have been in one of the cases behind the set of long, draped tables they were using as a phone and computer bank. Some workers were already there, blocking his view, getting set up to take phone bids and monitor the live online action. Chuck had seen it all.

What would Bob drink?

7

He strolled around Beverly Hills. It was too hot for his jacket but Chuck wanted to have class. Everything here was a clothes store. He saw a handbag the color and texture of a baby chick and thought of Shelly. The doors to one store opened as he walked past and a scent wafted out like the world's biggest perfume ad in a ladies' magazine. The window displays of Beverly Hills were freaky and oblique. Halved and mounted silver spheres. Looked like stuff you'd find in Bob Hope's house. Bob was ahead of the times. He had so much acrylic furniture.

Chuck imagined Bob drinking Campari and soda with Richard Nixon. He passed a vegetarian sandwich shop wedged into a corner and, some minutes later, a stray juice bar. Chuck was on the wrong street for booze.

He took some turns to a promising joint with weird architecture, winding and white. It was shaped like a corkscrew, or the famous California ghost house with the hallways that shrank and the stairways to nowhere. Inside was white too. Good, there was a bar along the back. A notable percentage of the lunch crowd consisted of strenuously tanned old men in the company of much younger women.

There was no bartender. Chuck sat at the empty white bar and checked out the shining bottles. Sparse and standard. This was not a place where people went for serious drinking. There were a couple of okay gins. A tattooed gal in a black tank top showed up to help him. He could tell she wasn't a bartender. She seemed to be juggling the whole place, "in the weeds," a phrase he knew from Shelly. He heard Shelly's voice saying it. Unlike Shelly, this young woman had never heard of a martini.

"You mean an *apple* martini?" she said. It seemed like a dated reference for one of her tender years. Chuck explained about gin.

The old man at the two-top behind him was telling his would-be starlet about roughage. "You don't need it; you're skinny," he said to her. Next thing you know, he was really doing that classic old chestnut about starting out in the mailroom, the one where his spunk got him into the office of the studio chief.

In the corner, alone, on a white leather banquette, a "faded beauty" was talking to herself.

Chuck felt kind of thrilled. But the server took the unopened bottle of gin somewhere out of sight. To secretly ask her manager how to make a martini? Chuck watched signs of frost vanishing from the waiting martini glass she had produced and abandoned.

He occupied himself considering the stem. Stems were different in California. This one was like two stems that arched away from one another, then joined at the top, leaving an ovular sliver in the middle. It was such an intelligent glass, but nobody knew how to pour a martini into it. The night before, he had downed a subpar, sticky-sweet Manhattan in the lobby bar of his hotel, and the stem had been like a prank you'd order from a comic book, curving away from the hand of the drinker, so you'd grab for it and it wouldn't be there. Your drink was floating in air with a breath of magic it didn't deserve. Were these stems a metaphor?

After a while Chuck left a fiver on the bar. He wasn't robbing her of trade. No one had been waiting for his barstool. But he left the money anyway because it was what Shelly would have done. Shelly was always kind to others whose position she had shared. She was always kind, period. Think of all those boys she had let feel her up. She had picked herself a lulu of a husband, a peacherino, a real dud. He felt himself rubbing his dry bottom lip like a drunk in a movie.

On the way out he saw the girl working the patio. She apologized like she was going to cry. He said consoling things.

8

When Chuck found the auction house again, the first person he saw inside was a slouched old professor lurching around in houndstooth. That's more like it, he thought.

They gave Chuck paddle 187, police code for murder.

He sat near the front, sweating like a pig in his blue velvet jacket, looking at that loose thread on his arm.

A nice couple sat next to him, the man in a baseball cap and camo shorts. His curly-headed old wife was dressed up and twinkling, all chestnut hair coloring and tasteful eye makeup and charming crow's feet and high pink cheeks. He liked seeing old guys with cool old wives. It didn't make him feel bad.

Behind him, two men had an affectionate discussion about their friend who had "died the right way, without a clue." One of them, changing the subject, said, "We had a dispute with a Japanese company." Like the geezer in the houndstooth, it was snug with his expectations. It was what he wanted to hear.

A sporty young fellow with ruddy cheeks and tousled golden hair arrived, a Dorian Gray type, or an older Tom Sawyer, or maybe Tom Sawyer grew up to be Dorian Gray. He talked to a woman in tinted glasses about an entire estate someone had consigned to him, and how he in turn had consigned it in parcels to various auction houses. He also attended auctions like this one to buy things for clients.

"I have literally shopping lists people give me," he said. "Literally, 'I want a thing that's horizontal with stripes.'"

The man in camo shorts—who, like Chuck, was eavesdropping—leaned forward and asked vaguely, "Are you a professional?"

"I wouldn't say that," the young man replied. "I'm an art advisor."

The man who had had a dispute with a Japanese company was describing in elaborate detail an old editorial cartoon about the Clinton sex scandal.

There was lots of teasing and laughing, a building, carnival energy as more people came in and time for the first gavel drew near. The art advisor struck up a fast friendship with Camo Shorts and his sweetly smiling wife. He moved back a row to sit next to them. He talked about the drab town where he had grown up ("Everything was olive") and how happy he was now.

Chuck counted twenty-one chairs in front of him, only three of them filled.

He looked behind him. The last two rows were completely full. Was there some advantage to being in the back?

The auctioneer rapped the crowd to order. His gavel had no handle. It was a hunk of wood he clutched in his fist. It was loud and scary but didn't seem to bother anyone. His expert banging accomplished nothing. People chatted on their iPhones, loose and rowdy, roaming around. The auction-house workers on their phones and computers were just as lively and loud. The family of the guy just in front of Chuck came in—wife and daughter, from the looks of them. They had a smelly doggie bag for their man. Civilization had collapsed, and this confident little rooster of an auctioneer with his pearly monuments of teeth was not going to save it. As the wife and daughter settled in, the husband and father gesticulated frantically about something and the auctioneer, who was taking bids on "two green lacquered Chinese-style game tables," paid him no mind at all. There were no quiet people in gray suits making tiny movements.

Chuck bid on an acrylic cocktail table, just to see what it felt like. It was terrifying. He raised his paddle for two fifty, but someone else must have bid at the same time, because the auctioneer looked straight at Chuck and called out three hundred. Chuck's heart jumped. It was fast, like losing money at roulette. He perceived that he was at the mercy of the mercurial auctioneer. As the price of the acrylic cocktail table went up he gave Chuck knowing looks and beguiling grins, trying to persuade him to shoot the works, openly giving the sucker the hard sell, not like the auctioneers in movies, who were dour as undertakers. Chuck felt it, he felt the sway, but kept his paddle in his lap.

Chuck had a thousand dollars he could safely spend. He meant to use it all on Donny's *Cancel My Reservation* pot if necessary. Yes, he would secure that first, then spend anything that happened to be left in the kitty on himself. He was already getting off track. Human greed, Chuck had it. The pot wasn't scheduled to come up for bidding until the next morning. Chuck shouldn't even have been in the auction house. He told himself it was research, a stakeout.

This is for you, Donny, came the grand thought.

He didn't flinch through the polar bear ice bucket and two Tiffany decanters, one etched with a facsimile of Bob Hope's autograph. He was stoic. This wasn't about him. Chuck had a higher calling.

The auctioneer worked it. He was a balding superhero, one of those little guys who pack a punch—Doll Man, Ant-Man, the Atom. The hair left him was darkly metallic and wavy.

He smoothed over his keen, professional aggression with jokes. Once there were some end tables no one was bidding on and he said in a mock wheedling tone, "Come on, it's Bob Hope!" Everybody laughed. But somebody took the bait.

He laughed too, and openly, at his task of making a Native American–themed golf award sound alluring. "That's unique: I didn't know Kachinas golfed."

For five chairs with upholstery so remarkably unappealing that the room fell silent in zonked-out awe, he said, "You can have four people over if you're single."

He was playing with their sadness.

A few lots later, in a searing flash of instantaneous buyer's remorse and what felt like incipient diarrhea, Chuck gave in and snagged some poorly punctuated linen bar towels (THE HOPE'S BAR, they said) and "two unmarked Far Eastern metal ashtrays."

Dizzy and guilty, brooding about what he had done, he had to step out for some air. The bamboo and wicker and rattan, forests of it, had begun to blur together.

Now he had absolutely no more than seven hundred dollars left to spend on Donny. Still, it was more than enough for the pot. Nobody would want that pot, would they? Why would anyone want that lousy pot? He sat on a low wall in the bleak, paved-over courtyard. People didn't care about Bob Hope. They were going for the furniture. "A lacquered animal hide console table with Asian style feet." What was that? It could have belonged to anybody. What were Asian feet? Well, they were something that had people peeling the big bills off their rolls. Memories, on the other hand, were cheap as dirt. Three C-notes for the ashtrays in which Bob Hope had personally stubbed out his cigarettes. And they came with Lucite coasters and glass toothpick holders thrown in. Nobody cared. Who but Chuck would bid on that gross pot from the spidery corner of Bob Hope's library? It would be a steal. Now Chuck had Bob Hope's bar towels and that's all there was to it. What's done is done, like buying a first-class ticket with no refund.

He poked his head back in the gallery. His auctioneer was gone. A lanky farm boy with a saucy forelock he kept pushing out of his face had taken his place. He was sepulchral and at the same time his voice would crack like an adolescent's. Maybe he was an apprentice. The main auctioneer sat nearby, resting and watching thoughtfully. The new guy seemed nice, but the spell was broken.

Chuck walked around Beverly Hills, killing time until it was late enough to get a cab to Maria's. At the corner of Beverly and Dayton, a passing guy asked his friend, "This is where that movie star committed suicide?" Or maybe he was saying it, not asking. That's how people said things, as Chuck had begun to notice. It wasn't his world anymore. He knew how Bob Hope felt.

9

It was somebody's birthday. Chuck never got a grasp on whose.

There was an NPR commentator who knew everything about tequila.

A woman in a scarf worked for a foundation.

A dignified person with a neatly pressed shirt and cotton-candy swirl of distinguished gray hair buttonholed a former scientist turned filmmaker (who kept calling himself "a former scientist turned filmmaker").

An otherwise nicely dressed man from Harvard walked around barefooted as an ape. Well, the guy had respectable feet. They were evenly ruddy, with smooth, glossy nails. They were too small for the guy, his feet were, but that made them even more precious. They were the feet of a faun. It was worse than going around naked. Chuck and Veda had been at a pool party with one casually nude guest and everyone pretended not to notice her coppery tuft glaring at them.

Chuck was out of his league. His feet were a disaster. He thought they were what kept him from falling in love again.

Maria gave everyone champagne to toast the elusive birthday. No, not champagne. "Sparkling wine," as she correctly said.

Maria lived down a mysterious winding lane that was gravelly and bereft of streetlights and seemed to split and double back on itself as it went along in deadly and unexpected hillocks. The cabbie had a tough time finding her house, which was a towering box of corrugated metal with an orange door. Chuck got out disoriented and stumbled around until he heard Maria calling to him from a balcony. Just feet away, the cabbie had pulled over and whipped it out to pee in the street. It seemed feasible. The dream road was loomed over by fantastic mismatched buildings, and worldly restraint didn't matter.

Sparkling wine hit Chuck's empty stomach. He kept proudly admitting he didn't know anything. No one was impressed by the saintly depths of Chuck's ignorance.

They were waiting for someone else to arrive before they could eat. It was killing Chuck. He was conscious of Maria's vibe from the other room, where she was slicing up tomatoes and stirring the pot. He wanted go in there and lean against a counter and catch up, maybe pick up something with his fingers and eat it. There was an open box of fried chicken just sitting there from a no-frills Korean place in a strip mall a few miles away. And Maria was tall and gorgeous, born in Vera Cruz. But somehow Chuck was tangled up in this sophisticated living room conversation, where the guy who knew everything about tequila made a speech describing each of the two hundred varieties of agave plant, only one of which could be used to make tequila. It seemed rude to get up and leave. Occasionally someone would squeeze in a word about his or her own fucked-up specialty.

Somebody said, "Of course, everyone thinks that Al Gore saved the world, but they're wrong."

Chuck guffawed. Guffawed was an accurate description. "Wait!" he said. "Wait! Wait! Everybody thinks Al Gore saved the world?" Then he said something like, "Haw, haw, haw." Everyone stared at him.

"Well, some of us lefties do," the woman in the scarf ventured at last.

Chuck had stepped in it. He was a lefty! Chuck was a lefty all the way. But he couldn't say it now.

The missing person showed up and the table was set.

Chuck fingered the gold threads in his pleasantly rugged napkin. Real gold, maybe. He had a thimble of the fine tequila the NPR man had brought. He wondered whether "notes of vanilla" would be a correct thing to say about it. He kept his yapper stapled.

Maria and the man with the wire-rimmed glasses and cotton-candy hair seemed to be in some kind of fancy wine club together—a club of two. Maria brought out a white wine she had been saving for him. It looked kind of brassy when she poured it.

"It's a funny color," said the thoughtful, quiet man, who was across the table from Chuck.

"It's old!" Maria said defensively. Chirped defensively.

The chicken was bleeding but Chuck didn't care. He sloshed himself a glassful of the rusty wine and started gulping it, only later stopping to think it wasn't for him. His tongue couldn't register how special it was.

Maria had made an incredible salad with raw corn.

"It was so sweet I didn't want to do anything to it," she said.

Chuck wished he could be like that, to know when not to do anything to some corn, to instinctively know that Christmas lights in different colors were "tacky" for reasons normal humans could never understand.

Maria sweetly tried to include him in the conversation, asking about the auction.

"Oh, ha ha, there was this horrible Leroy Neiman painting," Chuck said.

The quiet person across the table stopped him. "I happened to be at Leroy Neiman's ninetieth birthday party," he mouthed. "He was a sweet guy."

Chuck's soul froze up in horror.

"He's fascinating, of course," lied Chuck.

"Lee painted some real crap," said Leroy Neiman's friend.

"No, no," lied Chuck. "No, no."

"I was so privileged to be at his ninetieth birthday. You know, most of his birthday parties Lee invited only women."

The table chuckled at the venerable rascality of the incorrigible Leroy Neiman.

10

Maria had seemed excited about the auction. She had promised to be in Burbank by 9 a.m. sharp to pick up Chuck. He stood there waiting. A Ford Focus arrived. Someone stepped out of the driver's seat and peered. She was long-legged and dark like Maria, but much younger. She wore something fashionable that resembled a bellhop uniform from a 1960s science fiction movie. Chuck took one step in her direction. She examined him inquiringly. He pointed at himself. She raised her perfectly waxed eyebrows over her round black-lensed glasses in response. He crept closer to the car like a deviant.

"Are you…?" she said.

Chuck said he was Chuck.

"I thought so. Get in."

Chuck got in. So did she. She turned down the radio and put it in gear.

"Where's Maria?" said Chuck.

"She's sorry. She couldn't make it. She sends her apologies."

"Are you…?" said Chuck.

"Oh, I'm…"

"Are you her daughter?"

"Yes, that's exactly what I am. Angel." He realized that she wasn't calling him an angel, she was saying that her name was Angel. "Now, where are we going again?"

That morning the auction started with a pair of "Venetian Painted Blackamoors." Chuck apologized. "Bob Hope wasn't a racist," he said. "I guess everybody had some Venetian Painted Blackamoors."

"No bigs," said Angel. She was the understanding type.

"Will there be food?" she had asked him on the way. He had said no, so they stopped and he got her a breakfast burrito to go. But he was wrong. There was a pyramid of bagels and a much larger crowd than yesterday's attacking them. At the feet of the Ichabod Crane type next to Chuck languished a paper plate scattered with crumbs, a smeared black paper napkin, a plastic cup with a dribble of OJ left in the bottom, a torn cellophane peppermint wrapper.

Memorabilia seemed to be running higher today, and there was more energy, a wild rumble of nattering that never stopped. A fellow manning the phone table shouted like a revivalist, giving a spine-tingling "YAH!" or "YUP!" whenever an internet customer gained the top bid.

The *Cancel My Reservation* pot came and went in a breathtaking shaft of anticlimax, rocketing past him to $1,200. Chuck was astonished and crushed. Angel could see it. "You should have gone for that three-hundred-dollar little table that was really ugly," she said. "Or his old boot brush. That was a keeper." She found the whole thing amusing and, apparently, absurd. She was drawn nevertheless to a pair of lush, worn, burnt-orange velvet armchairs, susceptible as anyone to the intimate guile of the bantam auctioneer, though she dropped out quickly, shutting down his seduction with such deftness that Chuck could see the wonder and respect glimmer in his cagey eyes.

As the auction went on and Chuck made his bereaved and hesitant failures, she kept solemnly tapping the catalog photo of Bob Hope's grungy boot brush and raising her eyebrows suggestively. It worked every time and he couldn't help laughing, down as he was in spirit. She smelled like a bubble bath and made the hairs stand up on his arms. He couldn't think.

11

There was a lunch break between the morning and afternoon sessions. Angel and Chuck walked to a Beverly Hills deli with an aged clientele. He had chopped liver and explained things. The hours were running out. The last of the lots were coming up, and only a few remaining items would do for his sick friend. He couldn't afford a single distraction. His goal required all his concentration. Had she seen how expensive everything was today? It was crazy.

"I know, you kept saying, 'That's crazy!'" she told him.

"I did? Out loud?"

"Uh, yeah. Like nine times."

"How mortifying," said Chuck. "But I mean, somebody bought Bob Hope's Webster's Dictionary for two hundred dollars. It's a Webster's Dictionary. That's crazy."

"Well, you were really going for that shitty box," she said.

She meant the small crate of roughly joined planks, stamped all over with DANGER! LIVE INDIA MONGOOSE: THE SNAKE EATER. "When box is opened," the catalog declared, "a spring mechanism releases a furry tail and loud noise." It was listed adorably as "BOB HOPE NOVELTY TRICK BOX." Chuck was sure he had the only legitimate reason to bid on it, and found his deadened capacity for amazement jolted back to life when it swiftly rose in price and, like everything else, out of his range.

"You're getting this dude a gag gift, right?" said Angel. "So I think it would have been hilarious if you got him a gag. I mean, a gag gift that's a real gag? Hi-lare."

Chuck was bewildered and hurt. How was something from Bob Hope's home a gag gift? He hadn't thought of the box like that. He knew that Donny, lying there on his deathbed, would have gotten a real kick from handling this rare old piece of crude machinery that Bob had used to lay a cornball shock on the jaded partygoers of Palm Springs. Donny would think of some tough guy like Robert Mitchum whipping back his hand in fear and everybody having a snort of hooch and laughing about it around the old acrylic cocktail table. Chuck hoped it wasn't heart trouble, though Donny would appreciate going out that way, mortally stunned by Bob Hope's novelty trick box. Chuck had missed out on that frosted glass Christmas tree. It hadn't seemed worth paying attention to. But it came with a note from Mitchum, which Chuck had noticed too late. That old softie, that big lug, giving Bob a Christmas tree. Who would have expected such tenderness and sentimentality in such a mismatched pair? They were just like Chuck and Donny.

"A Bob Hope fashion award. That's a gag gift," Angel said.

Chuck couldn't explain to her why a Bob Hope fashion award, which indeed he had bid on for Donny, wasn't a gag gift.

"Do you even know who Bob Hope is?" he asked.

"Does it matter?" she said. "Hey, look. I have a friend who likes to dress up like a teddy bear and put on a diaper and wet himself."

"Okay," said Chuck.

"I drew a picture of him with a Hungarian flag as a diaper, and I posted it to my tumblr," said Angel. "I started getting all these angry comments, like, this is disrespect to Hungary or whatever. And I was like, 'Whatevs' or whatever. I was like, 'My friend is from Hungary and he loves this picture.' So you see?"

Chuck didn't see. He didn't see at all. She was speaking gibberish. Or he was. He looked across the booth at her and was flooded with feelings. It wasn't fair that Maria had to get older, replaced by this newer, firmer model, wearing clothes that might have been manufactured before Maria was born. People died and clothes lived forever? Something. Time had gone and got fluid on Chuck. He was one of those movie ghosts who doesn't realize he's dead until somebody points it out. His head swam and he must have looked a wretch. Angel reached across the table and touched his ghostly hand.

"The keychain was cool," she said, trying to make him feel better. He pulled his hand away.

"The keychain was *not* cool. Twenty-two hundred for a keychain. I'm starting to feel like there's something bad in the world."

"Any kind of membership card is cool," she said. "It said on it that all theater managers should extend every courtesy to Bob Hope and his party."

Chuck had to laugh, imagining Bob Hope fishing around in his pockets for his keychain so he could get into a movie for free. She really understood nothing about Bob Hope's place in the world. Soon she and her kind would be the only ones left on earth, a race of long-legged eternally youthful superbeings who smelled invigoratingly of soap.

"I have to go back alone," he said, signing the receipt for lunch.

"Well," she said, "give me a hug."

She stood up. He gave her a hug. He squeezed her too tight. He couldn't help it.

He watched her leave, a glimmering alien pharaoh's daughter parting a sea.

Chuck went into the deli bathroom, where he saw a stooped nonagenerian in a black suit. Chuck slipped past him into the stall and heard him out there knocking things over in big, chiming crashes. When he came out the old man was funereal as ever, bent over the sink, giving his crooked, lavender hands a slow and proper bath that never ended. Nothing Chuck could see was out of place.

12

The auction house was a riot of cold cuts. Why did Chuck keep missing the free food? He returned to his seat. Things tumbled from the mouth of the man seated just in front and to the left of him: particles of bread; the pale, curled sliver of a sickly tomato; two confetti scraps of lettuce. The sloppy eater turned around to stare, his irises so round and dark he looked like a cartoon character. Eventually, once the auction was underway again, he moved on. A worker in a dark blue uniform jacket cleaned up most of the mess. This place was like a soup kitchen.

Chuck dozed and had a vision of big ants crawling on a windowpane and a blue jay eating purple dragonflies, only its beak was broken. He woke himself up with a yell and found he was bidding on seventy swirled goblets, yellow and green. He bid some more. He drove up the price with what felt like horror and pulled out just in time to lose.

He glanced over minutes after losing a crystal ice bucket and saw it in the cabinet at the end of his aisle, so much smaller than he had thought, and wondered if he were really as coarse as he seemed, judging worth by size. In Atlanta in the early '90s, Veda had taken him to the birthday party of Ronnie Rude, a man with Down's syndrome who worked carrying ice in a bucket from table to table at the Clermont Lounge.

The Clermont was a kind of seedy club with weathered strippers who threw glitter and sang "Happy Birthday" to Ronnie Rude, and the glitter fell on the sad cake in the dark.

As its part of Atlanta had become gentrified, the Clermont had maybe turned ironic, a gag, a novelty trick box, maybe overvalued by nostalgists and underground purists, or maybe its reality was insulted by slumming yuppies from Buckhead. Now they were turning the adjoining flophouse into a boutique hotel. Veda would have been appalled. Supposedly there were plans to keep the Lounge intact—a living historical exhibit, the Colonial Williamsburg of despair. Chuck wondered what people were willing to pay for things, and why. He was fascinated by those who knew which kind of trash was the good kind, like Maria with her cheap but excellent bleeding fried chicken from a grimy storefront, and the authentic pig's foot he had seen bobbing around when she stirred her red beans and rice. It was a mysterious talent. Veda had always been very big on "authenticity," but Chuck hadn't thought about it much since she'd stopped being around.

He bid on a pewter ice bucket and remembered saying aloud while flipping through the catalog, "I don't know why people collect pewter." Now he did.

By the time the Baccarat ice bucket came along, he skipped it. He had developed ice bucket fatigue.

Behind him, a fresh and inexplicable crowd suddenly streamed in, greeting one another with excited squeals. He swooned in the hot jacket.

Around lot 576, a third set of Judith Leiber belts from the personal wardrobe of Bob Hope's wife, Chuck realized that he had entered a pleasant state of resignation, like freezing to death. He lazily smiled as he thought, *Wow, Dolores Hope sure liked Judith Leiber belts.* The woman in front of him bought some belts. The auctioneer had flashed his confident yet pleading grin at her. She was putty in his hands. Cruelly waiting for confirmation of an internet bid that would take the belts away from her, he snapped, "Chew faster!" The guy who yelled "YAH!" or "YUP!" was eating as he worked. Just jamming crackers in his mouth while he fucked with people's dreams.

They wouldn't even let Chuck buy Donny an "American Cinema Award." What in the hell *was* an American Cinema Award? Chuck could've given Bob Hope an American Cinema Award. It was so generic as to be totally meaningless. This auction existed because people burdened Bob Hope with piles and piles of crap wherever he went, to get an honorary degree in Utah or wherever. Stuff with his name on it, like diamond-studded belt buckles. Cufflinks and straps of leather emblazoned with his face. A Cross pen culminating in Bob's own miniscule head, plaques and bowls, melted-looking clay jugs, cheap trophies with detachable cowboys on top, frosted glass eagles and airplanes, Christmas ornaments and autographed globes, medallions and plaster busts, a barber pole. After a while it probably seemed more like a torture than an honor. They may as well have been gobs of spit flung in hateful rage, these treasures. Maybe it was a relief to die. The world is too full. Angel had been right about the Bob Hope fashion award, which Chuck had approached with a dumb earnestness that a member of her generation couldn't comprehend. The Nothing American Cinema Award for Nothing went for $2,500.

Then there were the clowns.

So many porcelain clowns.

"We should get Bob a clown, he's funny."

How many clown figurines had been unloaded on Hope by well-meaning dolts per year? Man lives to a hundred, he can accumulate a number of unwanted porcelain clowns. At some point he had so many that people really started to think he liked them, or so went the story Chuck told himself.

After half a dozen lots of clowns, the auctioneer said, "More clowns! What a shock," and got a nice ripple. *Sotto voce*, he leaned into the microphone: "How many more pages of clowns?" After that, people laughed almost dementedly, in a Pavlovian way, whenever he said "clowns," and finally that was just Chuck. Old Chuck laughed until he cried, barely keeping it together. Hey, maybe that was normal auction behavior. No one seemed to mind.

Chuck bought Donny some porcelain clowns. They were a gag gift. Angel had nailed it again. But there was a problem when Chuck tried to check out. The reception desk claimed that someone else had won Chuck's clowns.

He was so foggy he almost believed them. Harried superiors in headsets appeared. A chicly turned-out clerk rifled through accordion folders. At last it was determined that Paddle 188 had won the clown figurines.

"That could be a simple mistake," Chuck said. "I'm Paddle 187."

It looked as if negotiations were hopeless when the next person in line came up beside Chuck to engage a secondary clerk. This meticulous sport put down his paddle and Chuck saw that it was 188. The person who had been helping Chuck was ecstatic at the coincidence. She confirmed on the spot that Paddle 188 had not bid on the porcelain clowns. Chuck gave the guy a friendly nudge and said, "Ha ha, you almost got some clowns you didn't buy!" He was rewarded with a withering squint. Paddle 188 looked like the *X-Files* villain who enjoyed giving haircuts to corpses.

They brought Paddle 188 a book by Phyllis Diller, one she had signed to Bob. Paddle 188 opened it up and said, "Oh my God." Chuck glanced over and saw the full-page inscription in neat, packed lines of red ink, but couldn't read any of it before its new owner smacked it shut.

As Paddle 188 coolly appraised a crystal urn, Chuck went for his wallet and discovered it wasn't there.

"Oh my God!" he said. "I'll be right back."

Even as he crouched and searched his row, even as he started back for the deli, where his mind's eye placed his wallet on the smeared Formica, Chuck knew that Maria didn't have a daughter.

13

He begged them. They wouldn't fork over the clowns.

"But you have all my information already, from when I registered online," he said. "This is for a dear friend who's very ill. We don't even know how long he has."

They had no proof that Chuck was Chuck, they said. A nice security guard took pity, gave him forty dollars, and called him a cab. Chuck clammed up about how a couple of sawbucks wouldn't get him back to Burbank. He had the idea of crashing at Maria's instead.

He stood there waiting for the cab as the day gave way to brisk evening. The last stragglers emerged from the building, a large group all together. "Congratulations! You got some nice stuff," said a sassy, upscale person dressed all in white, with spiky platinum hair. Her friends probably called her "a little bundle of dynamite." She made him feel better with her electrically crackling eyes.

"I got some porcelain clown figurines!" he shouted. She and her friends were crossing the street and she looked back at Chuck with a puzzled expression. Then her crowd caught her up and they disappeared brightly down the block like the merry dead.

He turned to see Paddle 188 climbing into his cab, Chuck's cab, and shooting off down Bedford.

He was amazed when he turned to find that the windows of the auction house had been covered in brown paper, like a shameful package. It had been accomplished swiftly and silently, with marvelous efficiency. He found a side door and walked in.

"We're locking up," said the nice security guard who had helped him.

"I want everybody to know this is for Donny Billings," Chuck said.

There was a tasteful, narrow china closet with a flimsy-looking doorframe that housed a pointy trophy and some others. Chuck put his fist through the glass. Blood spurted wildly from his knuckles and wrist, splashed on the gold plate and the frosty Lalique.

Donny was going to love this.

Chuck held the three sharp prongs of the Las Vegas Entertainment Award in front of him like a dagger. Was it a crown or a jester's hat? Chuck made for the Neiman, right for its offensive mouth. He was going to wipe the smile off of Bob Hope's face.

They tackled him and zapped him before the damage was done. He felt the weight of a thousand bricks on his chest. He vomited up black stuff from his heart. It came out of his nose. His eyes rolled backward in his head forever.

He did not see his two dead wives making out with each other in Heaven, Bob Hope standing behind them, golf club slung scarecrow-style over his shoulders, winking in beatific lewdness.

He saw instead a montage of himself at liquor parties at which he had arrived with an empty stomach. He saw himself interrupting everybody and talking too loud and bragging about a famous punk rocker he knew. This was his life, the one that flashed. He saw himself with his greedy fist around a black plastic fork, cramming an entire serving of macaroni and cheese into his mouth at once. Decent people watched and could not believe their eyes.

Frosting Mother's Hair

TOM AND HIS MOTHER, MRS. WELLINGHAM, WERE PRACTICALLY THE same age. At fifteen, Mrs. Wellingham had married a twenty-year-old man—Tom's father—who was leaving to fight in a war.

Tom had grown up and gone off and become pretty wealthy in the soft drink business. These days he lived in a kind of semi-retirement. What he did, mainly, was fly around to different corporate retreats and present a lecture he had come up with called "Stop Having Fun in the Workplace."

Business had brought him back to his hometown after a long time away. Of course he went to visit his parents. Tom sat in a small living-room chair that seemed to have been crafted for a toddler. He wore one of his suits. He had just returned from lecturing a whole auditorium.

"What was the story about the root beer?" said Mrs. Wellingham.

"Which one?" said Tom.

"I think it's a wonderful story. I'm going to see some of the old gang soon and I want to tell them. Anne Marie is always asking about your work."

"I'm sorry. What story do you mean?"

"You said they really don't taste different, your brand and the other. I can't believe it."

"Well, now, that's true. It certainly is. It's quite a story, how that information came about."

"I have to get to the drag strip," said Tom's father, Mr. Wellingham Sr. He rose. Tom followed suit.

"Your father keeps strange hours these days," said Mrs. Wellingham.

"That's okay," said Tom. "I understand working for a living and pursuing what one loves."

Mr. Wellingham Sr. had finally sold the machine shop that had given him so much heartache over the years. Now he was a private consultant for a wealthy car collector. His job, as far as Tom could understand it, was making sure that suppliers of vintage car parts did not rip off his employer. And sometimes he lifted the hood of something and got his hands dirty for fun. He even drove a racecar as a hobby, despite his age. He won a lot of side bets from the smart young punks who thought they could take him. He and Mrs. Wellingham looked a lot happier these days, Tom thought.

"I need to fetch something," Mrs. Wellingham said. "I think it's going to be a delightful surprise. Now you two hug goodbye."

When she left the room, Tom and Mr. Wellingham Sr. stood there looking at one another.

"Your lady friend couldn't make it again, I see," said Mr. Wellingham Sr.

"Sam? Well, no. She bought two enormous stones and she's having them erected in the yard."

"Please don't tell your mother that. It would really hurt her feelings."

"I can't imagine why," said Tom.

But Mr. Wellingham Sr. was on to something. Sam was the main reason Tom hadn't seen his parents in two years. There was always something going on—her movies, for example, and big projects like her stones.

Sam couldn't understand why Tom would want to talk to his parents. She stood close by and mimicked him during his phone calls home. It was what made her special. She was only twenty-six. You never knew what she would do next. In a sense, though, she was probably jealous and acting out. Tom bought his parents nice things, such as the house they were living in now. They didn't want anything too roomy. They were alone.

Tom and his father said their goodbyes. Tom was still standing when his mother returned. She didn't sit down, so neither did he.

"Finish your story," she said. "I've promised lots of proud mother stories for my get-together."

"Oh, the taste test. Well, that was a long time ago. I'm not sure how interested your friends will be. They took us upstairs and blind-folded us for a lark. We had to admit that we couldn't discern our own product. There is actually more variation in separate batches of Mugsy than there is in the average batch of Mugsy versus the average batch of King Kevin."

"I just don't believe it," said Mrs. Wellingham.

"It's absolutely true, though our advertisements at the time stated the contrary. There is technically no difference in flavor between a bottle of Mugsy and a bottle of King Kevin."

"I still like Mugsy best, because that's your brand."

"It was," said Tom.

"And it really does taste better. You have too much faith in science and testing."

"Science is pretty reliable," said Tom.

"I wish I had a can of each in front of me right now," said Mrs. Wellingham. "I'd show you."

"Do you have something behind your back?"

"Yes, that's my lovely surprise." She revealed a box with a smil-ing woman pictured on the front. "It's something for us to do while you tell me your wonderful stories. You're going to help me frost my hair."

"Really?" said Tom. "I'm not sure that sounds feasible."

"I've been meaning to take care of it. I have a high school reunion coming up, as I was saying. Not a formal one. Just a group of us girls. But I'd like to look presentable."

"I'm not sure what frosting entails."

Tom's cell phone went off, a ringtone Sam had installed for him, some hip hop that embarrassed him in front of his mother.

"Jazzy," said Mrs. Wellingham.

Tom looked. Caller ID said it was one of Sam's friends. Unusual for him to be calling this number.

"Do you mind if I get this?"

"Why would I mind? I'm your mother!"

Tom answered the call.

"Tom? This is Barry Wick."

"Of course, Barry. Is everything all right?"

Barry was the director and sometime costar of Sam's films, in which Tom was often the principle investor.

"Don't worry, sir," said Barry. "There's no emergency or anything like that."

"Is Sam okay?"

"Yes, that's what I mean. Don't worry. I just had a quick question, if you don't mind."

"Well, I'll give the best answer I can. What's on your mind this evening, Barry?"

"I want to sleep in the same bed with Sam tonight. Fully clothed. It's nothing sexual."

"I'm not sure I follow you, Barry. I think you're going to have to clarify this one for me."

"Sam and I are collaborators, you know that. We really draw a lot from one another. There's a certain energy between us."

"Right…"

"That's it, really. I'd just like to hold her tenderly. All through the night."

Tom saw his mother looking at him. She had taken a seat and was holding the box of frosting in her lap. Tom turned away and faced the dim foyer.

"Uh-huh…" he said. "I'm afraid I'm not one hundred percent sold on this idea, Barry. It seems a tad intrusive."

"It's just the opposite, sir. We'd be fully clothed. I want to emphasize that. Look, I'm not going to do it without your permission. Sam didn't even want me to call."

"I see."

"But I thought it was important to get your input. To make you aware."

"Well, I certainly appreciate the thought."

"It's the thought that counts," said Barry.

"I'm just not sure that holds true for me here at this moment," said Tom.

"So what I'm hearing is, you're resistant."

"I believe that would be an accurate assessment," said Tom.

"I want you to know I'm going to take that into consideration as the night moves forward," said Barry.

"Thank you," said Tom. "I hope you will."

"I will."

"Terrific, then."

"Okay, I guess I'll be seeing you."

"Sounds good, Barry."

Barry was gone.

"What was that about?" said Mrs. Wellingham.

"Business," said Tom.

"You seem upset."

"I'm not," said Tom. "Where's that flatscreen TV I bought for you?"

"I put it in the guest bedroom."

"That's a funny place to put it," said Tom.

"I thought it would be nice to have this room just for sitting and talking."

"Sure, that's nice," said Tom.

"Come on and help me frost my hair. I want to involve you. You're home. My son's home. Althea used to do it."

"That seems more appropriate," said Tom.

"I'll put on my special poncho," said Mrs. Wellingham. "You'll love it!"

Mrs. Wellingham went into the other room again. When she came back she was wearing her special poncho. It was white, with bright dots on it that made Tom almost remember a picture book of his youth. Something about a shaggy creature with colorful spots. When he shook himself his spots got flung about. Something like that. It was hard to remember.

"We should go in the kitchen, over the linoleum, in case there's a mess," said Mrs. Wellingham.

They did so.

Tom's mother opened the box and laid out all the frosting equipment on the burnt-orange kitchen counter. It had come with the house, the counter had. Its color was of the 1970s. It should have been replaced.

"Noisome," said Tom.

"This is going to be a real ball," said Mrs. Wellingham. "Aren't we having fun?"

"Yes."

Mrs. Wellingham sat on a high kitchen stool. She put on a strange silver cap with holes in it. She tied a string under her chin to hold the cap in place.

"Do I look like a bathing beauty?" she said.

"Yes," said Tom.

She told him how to use the white plastic hook that came with the kit to pull strands of her hair through the holes in the cap.

"Just the holes with circles around them," she said. "I want an overall frosted look."

"It seems to me," said Tom, "that if you sincerely want an overall frosted look, you'd want your hair pulled through all these little holes, not just the ones with circles around them."

"I've been frosting my hair for many years," said Mrs. Wellingham.

"Very well. I'll defer."

Tom pulled some of his mother's hair through various holes.

"Just the ones with circles!" said Mrs. Wellingham.

"That's precisely what I'm doing," said Tom. "What makes you think I'm doing otherwise?"

"I raised you."

"Well, what on earth is that supposed to mean?" Tom put down the hook.

"Are you mad at me?" said Mrs. Wellingham.

"No. This happens to be exhausting. My wrist hurts. I believe the cap is defective."

"They wouldn't put a defective cap in the box."

"Is the cap supposed to have two layers?" said Tom. "It seems to have two layers. I don't believe the holes have been properly punched through the bottom layer."

"That's an illusion," said Mrs. Wellingham. "They have to make it hard for the gunk to soak through. Otherwise, there would be no precision. Your hair would be one big mess."

She picked up the hook and started pulling strands of her hair through the holes.

"What are you doing?" said Tom.

"I don't mind. It's not something you're used to. I understand. You've never frosted Sam's hair? I think she'd look darling with frosted hair. She and I could be twins!"

"Do you want a mirror? You're getting some of the holes without circles around them," said Tom.

"It doesn't matter," said Mrs. Wellingham. "Your new job is to tell me stories."

Tom told how he got his job almost by accident. Then he did the one about the day of orientation. They had been working right through lunch when one poor fellow brought a bottle of King Kevin into the auditorium with his sandwich. The instructor stopped in her tracks. The guy had purchased it from a vending machine on the very floor. Mugsy was leasing the building at the time, and they shared it with another corporation. In those days, the stocking of vending machines had been a lax industry. Mugsy had pioneered the stricter requirements that led to the advent of modern automated retail distribution branding. You wouldn't dream of finding a Pepsi casually stocked in the same machine with a Coca-Cola product, would you? Mugsy's innovation in that area had led the way, and it was probably all thanks to that poor dumb boob who had brought the King Kevin into orientation.

"And that poor dumb boob was me," Tom finished, as he always did.

"I can't do this anymore," said Mrs. Wellingham. "Let's just frost what we've got. Why don't you mix up the gunk? I'll keep pulling my hair through the holes until you're done."

Tom put on the plastic gloves. He took the two gunk packets over to the sink and mixed the contents in a little plastic tub. The fumes stung his eyes.

"It stinks of brimstone!" said Tom.

"It hardly smells at all," said Mrs. Wellingham. "They've made great improvements over the years. It doesn't smell nearly as terrible as a permanent wave."

When the gunk was ready to go, Tom came over and rubbed it on his mother's head. First he used the little spatula on the opposite end from the hook, as was illustrated on the instruction sheet, but it proved awkward, so he switched to a manual procedure with his gloved hands. He told his mother about all the foreign objects that had been found in bottles of Mugsy over the years, and the special division of the company that existed solely to investigate all such claims. He told of some celebrated cases in which fraud was proven, and some that turned out to be legitimate, such as the six baby opossums, and how the company had successfully hushed it up while still doing right by all afflicted parties, save for the opossums. He told her about all the trouble that Mugsy had been in with Third World countries. It was politically incorrect to sell a vacuous food item where people were starving to death. So Mugsy had come up with Mighty Mugsy Hercules, a beverage they sold only in Africa. A man could live on six bottles of Mighty Mugsy Hercules a day, and live quite comfortably—and get all his nutritional requirements, by the way. One day Tom's friend Danny had brought a bottle of Mighty Mugsy Hercules into the office and asked Tom to have a sip. It was terrible!

That was the funny part of the story, but no reaction was forthcoming. His mother had fallen fast asleep listening to the stories she had claimed to want to hear.

Tom didn't take it personally. He went into the pantry and got his father's wine. The bottle was almost full. Tom chose a big water glass from the drainer.

He walked into the dark, mysterious dining room and sat at the table. Things glinted at him from a china cabinet in the dark.

His father had always been a teetotaler, but after his friend Marty suffered a stroke, Mr. Wellingham Sr. had begun having a glass of wine every night, the way the medical community advised. Tom drank the wine and it made him think of his conception. The terrible honeymoon night of Mr. and Mrs. Wellingham was a traditional family tale. They had gotten into an argument because Mr. Wellingham was driving through town trying to get the car up on its two left wheels. Later Mrs. Wellingham had stormed out of the room and into the hotel bar, where she discovered a drink called the Tom Collins. It tasted like lemonade. Mrs. Wellingham had never had a drink up until that point, when she had ten of them. Had his mother even been conscious during Tom's conception? His father would have been cold sober. This was implication of the story that no one seemed to consider amid the merriment of the Thanksgiving table.

Once he had been at a party with Sam when one of her female friends started going on and on about her mother's problems with vaginal dryness. What kind of conversation was that? Tom stood there acting as if it were normal. Where did the girl get such information? From her own mother? Dear, dear.

"I hate my mother," Sam had contributed at that time.

He tried calling Sam. She didn't answer. He had seen her in the act of not answering her phone when people called, people she found distasteful.

Once Barry Wick had asked Tom where he was from, and Tom had told him. Then Barry Wick said, "Wow. That sounds real huckleberry."

What did that mean? It seemed designed to make Tom feel like a fool. Tom didn't know what to say. Barry Wick had a nice smile on his face. Was it a friendly remark?

There was an undertone of hostility, Tom thought, but he couldn't be sure. He still considered it from time to time. It occurred to him that maybe it was something Barry Wick had been saving up to say for a long time, a new piece of slang he had overheard or invented, a line he wanted to try out, and Tom had provided him with a good opportunity. If true, this theory would make Barry Wick a very shallow person, more concerned with how he came off in other people's eyes than with any real content of his own soul.

What about the time Sam had hiked her skirt and peed in a parking garage? At the time it had seemed bold. You never think about how much a person pees at one time until you see it spread out on the concrete. It looked like a map of North America. What had Tom found so commendable? Sam and her friends had made a cultish virtue of behaving like infants.

In their movies, Sam and her friends had a lot of dialogue about how life was about to change because they were turning twenty-four or something. One day they would be twenty-seven. They shook their heads at the thought. In Sam's movies, every character was worried about turning twenty-seven. Then they stripped off their clothes.

Often there was a foolish character, a boss or some other authority figure, played by a young man of thirty or so—an ancient. He told boring stories. He talked and talked and the protagonists rolled their eyes behind his back or dozed off.

A sudden, vivid memory was triggered. Tom couldn't make a conscious connection, but there it was, from back when he had first joined the Mugsy Beverage family, oh my gosh, twenty-five years ago. He had been considerably younger than Sam was now, but with so much more responsibility.

His first convention. New Orleans. Everyone was having vodka drinks and rice wine and malt liquor and BC Powder and something called a hurricane that tasted like fruit punch. Everyone was combining each of these things all at once. The drunken mother of one of his coworkers showed up, which didn't seem entirely professional. She appeared to be interested only in the free food. The free food was all she could talk about until she grabbed Tom and said, "Do you know who you look like?"

"No, ma'am," said Tom.

"You look like that little squirt on that famous TV show," said the drunken mother of Tom's coworker.

There were a lot of people standing around, listening. Tom tried to think of something smart to say but he was only a young man.

"Thanks, I guess," he said.

"No, it's a compliment," said the woman. "He's going to make a cute little man when he grows up. But your parents didn't do you any favors when they didn't have your teeth fixed."

If Tom's mother had been there, she would have said something quiet and gracious, and her simple, nonjudgmental tone would have made the other woman ashamed.

Tom was glad he had a nice mother.

Over the years, the incident would pop into his head and he would try to think of what he should have said instead of standing there with egg on his face. The best he had come up with so far was, "At least I'm not an old drunken slattern."

Sometimes he even let himself think that maybe the old drunk had a point. Why *hadn't* they done something about his awful teeth? Now he wore the braces that Sam had talked him into. They hurt all the time.

Tom finished the wine. He took off his shoes and padded through the kitchen, where his mother was still nodding on the tall stool at the counter. It didn't look safe, quite, but he wasn't sure what he could do about it. He couldn't pick up his own mother and carry her to bed! There were two more bottles at the back of the pantry. Terrible stuff. Wine from Oklahoma. He opened one of the bottles and drank a good bit of it in the guest bedroom, where he stared at the flatscreen TV, which, as he could plainly see, had never been taken out of the box. Eventually, he passed out.

Tom was shaken awake by his father, a big man with familiar hands.

"What have I come home to?" Tom's father said.

Tom could hear his mother crying in the other room.

"We're taking your mother to the emergency room," said Tom's father. He pulled Tom to his feet.

Tom lay in the backseat with the back of his hand against his slick forehead, blearily watching the streetlights' swoop, and the moon, which seemed to stay in the same place as his father swept through the traffic, an expert. His mother had stopped crying so much about the chemical burns on her scalp and spoke with some courage about what fun it would be to buy a hat.

Your Cat Can Be a
Movie Star!

NO MATTER HOW I SEARCH MY MEMORY, I CANNOT RECALL WHEN
Sandy Baker Jr., bartender at the Green Bear, first mentioned
in passing that his cousin in Hollywood was a high-level "animal
wrangler"—a gruesome phrase for a noble profession!

Have you ever enjoyed the sight of a chimpanzee on roller skates
and wearing human clothing in a motion picture? Perhaps the chimp
has donned a beanie as well, and the brightly hued plastic propeller
on top spins around and around as he skates merrily along.

You would be a heinous prevaricator of the highest order or else
a withered misanthrope with a heart of stone were you not moved to
the loftiest realms of entertainment by such a sighting of the playful
primate in question. It is a little known fact I read in a magazine or
saw on TV that Clint Eastwood's highest-grossing film is not one of
his brooding contemplations on the nature of violence and the decay
of the body, but the one with the orangutan who gave everybody
the finger. It is a mark of the popularity of such films that I recall
the orangutan's name as Clyde, whereas my brain has retained no
memory whatsoever of the name given to Clint Eastwood's character who liked to hang around with Clyde.

Now, how do you think the chimpanzee (or in Clint Eastwood's
case, orangutan) who has given you so much joy got to work that

day? Did he ride the bus? It is highly unlikely, though I have no doubt a chimpanzee could be taught to count out correct change for bus fare.

You guessed it! Mr. Buttons (for that is what we will call our hypothetical chimp "chum") arrived to the set right on time, his grateful belly freshly filled with ripe bananas, thanks to the tireless efforts of an animal wrangler.

That's all well and good for the ape family, comes the logical rejoinder. *I imagine an ape or a monkey could be a real handful. But what about the spider in* Annie Hall? *They probably just found a spider walking around on the ground.*

Wrong again, on several counts. First of all, there is no spider in *Annie Hall*. I believe you are referring to the eminently touching scene in which Diane Keaton would like to get back together with Woody Allen after a breakup. She calls him on the phone, weeping, and tells him about a large spider in the bathroom. An amusing scene follows in which an outmatched Woody Allen, armed with a tennis racquet, attempts to vanquish said spider, which he describes as being "as big as a Buick," using the humorous methodology of hyperbolical speech. The spider, however, is never seen. Characteristic of Woody Allen's filming techniques, Mr. Allen is visible only in part through a doorway, his frantic, half-obscured motions indicating his mammoth struggle with his arachnid foe, probably to save money on animal wranglers. For yes, a spider would have required a spider wrangler, as amazing as that may sound.

In Europe there are no animal wranglers, which is why every European movie has a scene that starts with a live duck getting its head chopped off. They don't build up to it with some dramatic music that goes dum-dum-DUM. There might be a couple smooching or some people walking in a field, then BANG! A duck getting its head chopped off.

There is a reason no one wants to know "how the sausage is made." How the sausage is made is terrible.

Let's get back to this spider for a minute, you may understandably insist. *It concerns me that an animal can be implied in a movie. How do I know that Hollywood will make room for my cat, whom I wish to turn into a movie star, if they are so big on leaving everything to the imagination? In fact, isn't the pioneering 1940s horror movie named after cats,* Cat People, *all about what is left* off *the screen, in the darkness of the viewer's imagination?*

Fair enough! But there is good news concerning your cat's movie star potential. For you see, a cat is often used as a *substitute* for the darker forces being explored. In other words, you can imply a spider, but a cat *is* the implication, and therefore cannot *in itself* be implied. Is there a murderer lurking about? Then certainly a cat will knock over a garbage can and give everyone a scare. This happens in *Pickup on South Street* and numerous other films. Even in *Cat People*, which you mention, an innocent kitten serves as visual counterpoint to the mysterious and otherworldly "Cat Lady," who is never exactly seen except in her sultry and all-too-delectably-human form. Did you know that actress dated George Gershwin? He was a lucky guy! Until he died of an agonizing brain tumor just at the prime of his young life.

Movies would be nothing without cats, whereas spiders (with the notable exception of *Kingdom of the Spiders*) are almost wholly dispensable. Even the greatest movie spider of all is never seen. Do you recall, in *Through a Glass Darkly*, when Ingmar Bergman's heroine reveals that God crawled on her face and He was a horrible cold spider? Of course you do! Well, we never saw that spider, did we? To see it would have defeated the point. There is no way any individual spider is going to become a movie star.

Most of my conversations with Sandy Baker Jr. on this admittedly inexhaustible subject must have occurred at some point in my enjoyment of the fruits of his labors as a bartender. Nor was the relative viability of various animals breaking into the film industry the only subject upon which he proved to be a perceptive and appreciative sounding board. I recall telling him about my idea for a children's book about Scriabin. I imagine the conversation may have gone like this:

"Who's this Scriabin character?"

"As a young boy he used to kiss and hug his piano."

"If you say so."

"He was a visionary composer who wanted to bring about the end of society with his cataclysmic music."

"How'd that work out?"

"Before he could finish, he picked at a pimple on his face and the next thing you know he was dead of gangrene."

Sandy took to calling me "The Old Idea Man," and hinted that he, by contrast, was a man of action. He put such wild things in the air as the veiled suggestion that he had once had to eat part of his own body to survive.

Well, this guy is obviously full of beans, comes the swift judgment.

You didn't know him, with his compelling line of talk and wet, hypnotic eyes.

No, he was no buttoned-down milquetoast, scared of braggadocio. Is that what you want in an advocate? I knew from the start that Sandy Baker Jr. was a volatile type, the sort of person who in the worst-case scenario becomes a petty demagogue or tells his followers to eat poison so the UFOs can come get them. I was warned about him.

As may be imagined, the old farmer who frequented the Green Bear tavern was stoic and in tune with the cycles of nature. Naturally, he was wary of people from the "me generation" or "generation X" or the "flower people" or "young rowdies" or "potheads" or whatever it was that Sandy Baker Jr. apparently represented to him. I should have guessed as much. I suppose I was fooled by my own image of the bar as an oasis full of the cheerful barbs characteristic of masculinity as it is practiced in the United States and on the classic sitcom *Cheers*. It is instructive to consider how many times the character Cliff Clavin would have committed suicide in real life had he been subject to such bullying as he endured on that show.

One evening I took my customary walk to the bar a little later than usual. As I recall, twilight was in the air and the weather was cooling nicely. My wife was out of town for work and I felt some mild and pleasant sense of liberty.

A stranger (to me) was tending bar, a gruff bald man replete with misshapen teeth in sore need of a dentifrice. Some younger people were milling about, a few in lab coats, refugees from the local chemical plant. Sometimes a familiar place can seem like a different world.

At least I saw one of my fellow "regulars," the old farmer, and I was moved by sentiment. I had never before had the courage to simply sidle up directly next to him on a stool and engage in casual chitchat, but suddenly I found myself not only willing but eager to do just that, my lonely feelings due to my wife's absence intensified and supplemented by the natural impulse toward "male bonding."

To my astonishment, the old farmer was garbed in a gray pinstripe suit, a far cry from his usual dungarees or overalls. I fear that my opening remark was some jovial observation on the subject.

"My friend died," came his sobering reply.

He was referring to Ned Brick, the old detective with whom he had so often gambled.

We spoke for a while of sad things, such as a trip to Alaska he had always hoped to make with his first wife but never had.

The old farmer had been a pallbearer at the old detective's funeral. I speculated aloud at one point as to whether Sandy Baker Jr. had been similarly employed. This the old farmer answered with a grunt.

I made some remark about Sandy, something about how he didn't seem so bad to me, a half-hearted defense, I must admit, because at the moment my most cherished hope was that the old farmer would like me. We are always going around criticizing St. Peter for denying Jesus thrice before the crowing of the cock, but come on! It is so easy to want to "go with the crowd" who happens to be around. We all just want to fit in.

"You must know about my disappointing, fat son," the old farmer said.

I was startled in numerous ways. For one, it seemed that a very personal conversation was about to ensue. Also, it was intriguing to think what association Sandy Baker Jr. might have with the old farmer's disappointing, fat son. Also, it seemed to be a terrible way to describe one's son. Also, there is the matter of my own weight.

I noted that the old farmer was drinking gin, a harder libation than usual. On the spot I made the mental decision to recall his every word as closely as possible, and to use the lengthy restroom breaks for which he was so justifiably famous to make some notes in my own form of shorthand, which I planned to transcribe in my leisure at home. As you will see from the following, my plan was a success in that regard.

"You're telling me you never heard of my fat, disappointing son? His name is Shell."

I paused to think. It is true that I had heard the name Shell mentioned somewhat frequently, though I could not recall in what capacity. I had a nagging sense that the Shell of which I had heard was a woman, or had been talked about in strictly womanly terms. I was amazed to think that this Shell of my imaginings could be a male of any kind. I thought it best not to mention this, and merely shook my head as if in blankness.

Shell, I was informed, blogged constantly about a young actress named _____. I leave the name blank not from pretension or postmodernism, but simply because the old farmer could not remember the name of the actress that his son liked to blog about. Otherwise alert people of a certain age begin forgetting the names of current superstars, and why shouldn't they? This man probably knew everything about the phases of the moon.

From various clues, I would suspect that the old farmer might have been trying to refer to Scarlett Johansson, due to a number of mentions of "red hair," though I cannot say so with certainty. Ms. Johansson has been viewed in films with various shades of hair, red certainly among them. Perhaps a certain jpeg from Shell's blog, at which the old farmer had gazed with disgust, had fastened itself to his mind with, dare I say it, the strange admixture of lust and distaste that is so common for all of us who participate in humankind.

Shell was fifty years of age, and the old farmer found it unseemly that the girl of his obsession still had baby fat on her, in the old farmer's estimation. This also makes me suspect that her identity was that of Scarlett Johansson, who is a person so soft and creamy, resembling nothing so much as a nourishing bowl of oatmeal.

Hypocrisy! cries the alert reader familiar with the area and its inhabitants. *Isn't this the same old farmer who has a child bride named Cherry of all things, covered in pale, pink freckles from head to shapely toes?*

To which I can only respond, "Touché."

But may I suggest that we pause before rushing to judgment and take a hard look at our own lives and impulses? It is probably far from uncommon that we recognize as great sins the small faults in others that we fail to recognize in ourselves.

Not that there was any sin involved, on the face of it, with the marriage of the old farmer to his legally aged wife Cherry. As I brood on this complicated matter, it occurs to me that what really bothered the old farmer was his son's timidity. Shell was not going after his dream! Rather than tracking down Scarlett Johansson (for the sake of argument) and asking her on a date, he was content to scan the Internet for candid photographs of her, in effect building a virtual shrine to her in full view of a disbelieving public, at which he could kneel and worship like a wretched mooncalf.

One warm evening the old farmer came home, or so he related, after dropping off his young wife Cherry at the airport, to notice that the living-room furniture had been pushed against the walls. Next he saw Sandy Baker Jr. with his shirt unbuttoned all the way. Sandy Baker Jr.'s ribs were prominent and pronounced and his chest was quite hairless, almost as if denuded by artificial means. As another part of this scenario, the old farmer's middle-aged son Shell was on his hands and knees. Sandy Baker Jr. was riding Shell around the room like a horse.

Have I mentioned that Shell was living with Cherry and the old farmer at the time, due to his pending divorce? Naturally, the old farmer wished to ascertain what was "going on."

"I was showing Shell here some tricks," Sandy Baker Jr. offered, buttoning his shirt, having dismounted, and attempting to make himself look presentable under the circumstances.

The old farmer thought of a postcard that Cherry had mailed him from one of her shopping trips to Dallas, showing a spider monkey in a cowboy outfit riding a large dog. At the time, everyone had said it was "cute" and "funny." But now he remembered with stark immediacy the grim, desperate faces of the monkey and the dog.

As he told his story, the old farmer had been staring into the filthy mirror behind the bar, staring the way he might have stared at a fallow field, full of longing and knowledge, seeing things a layman could never see. Suddenly he turned those burning eyes on me.

"Stay away from Mr. Sandy Baker Jr. He'll beguile you with his powers, and soon you'll be his henchman on his bloody, hidden deeds."

This was interesting news, because I had recently given Sandy Baker Jr. the sum of $300 that didn't exactly belong to me so that he could have some special publicity shots of my cat made up.

Inspired by the old farmer's newfound passion for gin and the reluctant thought of returning to my own dark house, I consumed a quantity of Gibsons and made many embarrassing proclamations, only a few of which I can recall with any certainty, most if not all of them to uninterested strangers.

A basketball game came on the TV, and as the national anthem was being played I arose with a ceremonious air and hoisted my conical glass and the three wondrous white onions impaled on a toothpick within to the beautiful young woman singing and the enormous flag held parallel to the ground like a safety net by a contingent of artfully arranged Marines. I became belligerent afterward because no one else had stood. "I guess I am the only one standing up for a lady," I am afraid I declared. "A lady called America!"

At another blurry juncture, I tried to persuade the frightening bartender to turn over the personal telephone number of Sandy Baker Jr. In retrospect, it should have given me a clue to his nature that Sandy was so secretive in his refusal to reveal those very digits, which should have been tucked in my wallet seeing that we had become business partners of a sort and even partners in crime, for what had I done but robbed my wife's company under her very nose, like a mastermind for whom the FBI agent in charge of the case develops a grudging respect?

Yet thank goodness the fearsome barkeep did not comply! I was left bereft of the contact information I so assiduously sought.

What a condition I was in: drunken, combined with doubts and anger. Given the volatility of my intended communicant, I cannot imagine that the confrontation would have gone well.

What if I had used Sandy's number as a means of finding his address? What if I had gone over to his apartment or hovel and banged on the door in a rage?

In one such imagining I am pinned to a wall by the projectile of a crossbow and my body, once pried free with some difficulty, is dumped in the old farmer's catfish pond, along with so many others. I suppose most catfish are farm-raised now, and it is a good thing. They are awful creatures, monstrous to gaze upon, and will eat anything, including my remains. To name a thing like that after its supposed resemblance to a cat is the gravest insult. I hope you do not have a pet catfish because chances are he will never be a movie star! Ha ha!

I should pause to admit two things:

1) Sometimes I call my cat "Catfish" as a nickname because of her cute little puffy fish face.

2) There is a movie called *Catfish* and for all I know it has a catfish in it. We should all be more scrupulous and not fling around generalizations with abandon. Why am I imagining a catfish circling and circling in a cheap inflatable wading pool? Is that something I read about in a review of the film? A catfish is possessed of extremely sharp and painful cartilaginous (I guess) "whiskers." Anything inflatable, which might be endangered by harsh poking, would be an unwise container for a catfish. Perhaps that is a central metaphor of the movie, the folly of keeping a catfish in a rubber wading pool. I have not seen it, so I hope I am not giving anything away. Somebody apparently put his catfish in a movie long before my cat became a movie star, so hats off to that enterprising gentleman (or woman). The more I think of it, the less can be said with any certainty on any subject whatsoever. My tongue is a small sea creature indeed, thrashing about so crazily in the hull of an enormous fishing boat christened *Ignorance*. Wittgenstein was right when he philosophically told us all to shut our big kissers for good. I believe that wily old German

went so far as to say that we shouldn't even make pronouncements like, "The sun will come up tomorrow." But just try telling that to Little Orphan Annie. Who said that Wittgenstein is necessarily right about everything all the time? Why shouldn't we say, "The sun will come up tomorrow"? What if it doesn't? In that case, we will have lots of worse things to worry about than what we said about the sun yesterday. In actual fact, what we say about the sun has very little effect on the sun at all.

When I thought about what to say to Sandy Baker Jr., not every outcome I considered ended with me dead, a clunky bolt shot through my throat.

I also imagined that I might murder Sandy Baker Jr. in self-defense.

What if he came at me with his crossbow raised? What choice would I have but to pick up the novelty "lava lamp" I imagine he would have sitting on an end table for irony? I might smash the lava lamp in his face, releasing its scalding contents, which would blind him. Or perhaps a shard of it would sever one of his arteries. Were it still plugged in, it might well electrocute him.

Thank goodness, then, for the professionalism of the reticent yet ugly bartender. A bartender is used to receiving many slurred requests, few of which he fulfills, unless they involve a fresh drink. That is as it should be. One thing we can be content to know in this world is that we can count on most people to do their jobs in good faith.

One thing from which the unattractive if dedicated service professional could not save me was a wretched hangover. When one's spouse goes out of town, the initial thought is, "Welcome back, bygone days of bachelorhood. I may as well loosen up and have some wholesome fun!" The reality always ends in pain.

Upon my wife's return, I managed to choke out a catalog of my misdeeds.

For business purposes, she has been endowed by her employer with an American Express card devoid of any limit. With it, she pays for meals and necessary sundries on business trips. She then files an expense report to the accounting office. Once it has been approved, a check is issued. My wife deposits the check and uses the funds to pay off her corporate American Express card in a timely manner.

Potentially limitless funds! You can see the unfortunate temptation for a spouse who wishes to turn his cat into a movie star.

I regret to say I "borrowed" my wife's corporate credit card without her knowledge. It was with an excess of adrenaline that I met Sandy Baker Jr. at the prearranged spot: a particularly shabby and generic automatic teller machine near a diseased tree.

My hands were quaking as I slipped the stiff rectangle of fiduciary plastic into the appropriate slot. The source of said quaking was twofold: first, what right had I? Could my actions get my wife fired, or even jailed? Second, my attempt at entering the personal identification number represented the sheerest of guesswork. Perhaps an entirely random number had been assigned by my wife's company. I chose to assume, however, that this card shared the "PIN" of all our other cards and accounts. (An interesting side note: I almost just told you what it is before deleting it! That is how at ease I feel with you, dear reader, with whom I share so many dreams and goals. But that is no reason to throw caution to the wind entirely, as I am sure you will agree. Suffice it to say, the number bears a poignant romantic association for my wife and myself.)

Luckily (or unluckily) my marital instinct paid off to the tune of three hundred big ones. Sandy Baker Jr. could not possibly have been more delighted.

In contrast, my wife's response to this tale was not a good-humored one.

"You've never kept secrets from me," she said. After a pause, she added, "Have you?"

I suddenly realized what my breach of trust had done! It had thrown everything good and true into question.

She was also upset because a credit-card payment was imminent, and where was this extra money supposed to come from? She did not say it, for she is the least cruel of persons, but the implication—whether intended or not—was that no extra money might be had from any source, thanks to my unemployment and despair.

"Let me get this straight," she said. "You let this vagabond into our *home*? And he took pictures of our cats? What else did he take? Do I need to inventory the china? I can't believe you let this character near our *cats*!"

I tried to soothe her by explaining that Sandy Baker Jr. had never set foot over our sacred threshold, that our feline transactions had been entirely digital in nature and had involved just one of our cats—the one that seemed destined for movie stardom. I had sent him a wide selection of good photos of our potential movie-star cat over Facebook. He needed the money in order to have them printed out on the proper high-quality photographic stock expected in Hollywood, with the required amount of "resolution" and "pixels," and a professionally "pumped-up" kitty résumé printed on the back in an acceptable font. Multiple copies and shipping costs were other considerations. We had both agreed after some deliberation that Priority Mail with an official notification of receipt was the way to go.

My wife was having none of it. "I don't like it when somebody takes advantage of my sweetie," she said. Her brown eyes flashed with exciting danger! She expressed her idea that we should "march right down to that bar" and demand the money back.

I begged her to reconsider. I was willing to admit that maybe Sandy Baker Jr. had made a fool of me. But I could not stomach the idea that my foolishness—if such it was—might be made manifest in front of the crowd at the Green Bear, of which I had come to think as a kind of peaceful sanctuary. From what? That is a difficult question. Not from home, surely, where my cats and wife reside. From life? Better not to spend one's life in constant analysis, as proven by the bestseller in which Malcolm Gladwell tells us, "Just do things without thinking about it like the great geniuses of history, who never thought about anything, and soon enough you will be a genius like me (and by implication, your cat will be a movie star if you have one)." Action! Action is the key.

"We could invite him over here," I said.

"That's it!" my wife agreed. "Under some pretext."

My expression revealed that I did not know quite what she was getting at.

"And he was never seen again," she said.

We laughed, enjoying my wife's dark sense of humor.

"We could invite him over to dinner," I said. "Keep it private and friendly."

"And if he doesn't fess up, then *whack*!" my wife said. "Hold on."

She left the dining room, where we had been seated, and I heard her going down the hallway to our bedroom, one of the cats humorously following and making a cute little sound characteristic of it: *myuh-myuh-mew-M'YOW!*

I felt my capillaries become chilled with fright. I knew what she was going after. And sure enough, she returned, slapping it methodically against her palm: an old-fashioned policeman's "sap," its leather glowing a deep, warm black with age.

"Nobody messes with my sweetie," she said.

I beg your pardon. Do you know what a sap is? It is a small, light instrument for concussive purposes, a deceptively sweet-looking little club with lead concealed in the "business end." You would not wish your tender brains to come up against one! This particular weapon my wife kept under the bed in case of intruders. It was an antique, belonging to her great-grandfather, a beat cop in Mobile, Alabama, who died of a heart attack at an extremely young age one day as he pounded his beat. There are a number of fascinating stories about him, particularly his death and its aftermath.

Oh, this is just what we need, groans the burdened reader. *Genealogy. I reckon it is the only subject we haven't covered yet in this tedious encyclopedia of human knowledge in its cosmic entirety.*

To which I would counter with what has been proven again and again in many major studies: writing is at heart a therapeutic practice, meant to make the writer feel better. How often as a teenager did you scrawl a poem in your loose-leaf notebook, just to get something off your chest? Can it truly be that you have lost your sense of youthful innocence? If your main hope is to turn your cat into a movie star, you should hold such feelings tightly to your breast.

As we grow older, and some of our hearts grow bitter, closed, and frigidly cold, we turn to the writing of others, hoping that some of the therapy will rub off. It is in that spirit that I hope you will indulge me.

No, I was going to tell you a lot of things, such as when the cop climbed up into the attic a week before his death and saw his deceased first wife stretching out her arms toward him, but now I don't feel like it anymore.

"If he doesn't come clean, we'll knock him out and roll him," my wife said. "I hope his skull isn't too thin."

I knew she was speaking in jest, but there was an underlying seriousness at play. Back when I was working, I would often tell my wife of some perceived slight done to me in the callous wording of an e-mail.

"They'd better be glad they're in another state," she would say. "I'd kick their asses."

This sort of rough talk coming from my gentle spouse had always made me smile. At the same time, I had always sensed that the fierceness of her loyalty was no joke, a fact which filled me with deep and unending satisfaction.

The next time I saw Sandy, I invited him over to dinner. I behaved as my wife had suggested, with no hint at all of her suspicions. I used the reason she had concocted: that he needed to meet our cat in person, the better to "sell" her unique talents and personality to his cousin the animal wrangler.

"Funny you should mention that," he said. "Those pictures didn't work out. I should bring over my special camera that has the right amount of pixels. We'll do a little fashion shoot with kitty kitty."

"She's shy if you don't know her," I said. "So you didn't end up using those pictures I sent? Maybe I should get my money back so we can reinvest it in other opportunities along these same lines."

"Well, no, bro, it's not like that. I already shelled out for the special-order materials, didn't I? And I sent some of the goods out to Glendale already, to my cousin's office out there. I can't help it if he tore them in half. He says we got just one more chance to make good, so we really have to shoot the works this time, do it up right, impress the hell out of him, show him we're not just a couple of country rubes, that we know you have to spend money to make money. Speaking of which, I'm out a good bit of money on this deal already."

"I'm sorry," I said.

I was also sorry that I couldn't get the money back from him, because that would have gone a long way toward easing my wife's concerns.

I still had hope. If there is one thing you learn, it should be "Keep Hope Alive." Sandy Baker Jr. might still have been on the up-and-up as far as I was concerned. He certainly had a lot of details on the tip of his tongue, such as the authentic-sounding word "Glendale."

I knew that my wife's hope, counter to his, was to shame him into admitting he had "conned" us. I knew that *his* hope was to talk my wife out of more money. I admit I was torn. Really I wanted my wife to be convinced, so I could continue to be convinced, so we could be convinced together. Sandy Baker Jr. was a good convincer. He was the man for the job, I thought. I just wanted everything to be easy.

But everything is not always easy.

On the Saturday that Sandy Baker Jr. was to come to our place for dinner, I set about my housework like Cinderella herself, sure to get at every spot with my duster, my broom, and my mop. My wife, who normally felt the urge to tidy up before company arrived, did not share my enthusiasm on this occasion. She remained in bed, enjoying the melodramatic domestic dramas of the Lifetime Network, while I sat at the computer, my chores completed, my chicken simmering, and devised a new iTunes playlist of background music which I felt sure would be to Sandy Baker Jr.'s liking, though we had never discussed his tastes.

When the knock came on the door, my wife emerged, and I was a little dismayed to see that she had not changed out of her lime-green sweatpants, stained T-shirt with a garish flower on it, and old cloth robe. Overall, she appeared tousled and uncaring. To me, of course, she remained the most beautiful vision in existence.

Sandy Baker Jr. held out a bottle. "You can only get this sh** in Chicago," he said. "It's godawful."

"How thoughtful," my wife said. She had some snideness coming through, which was on purpose. She read from the label. I can't recall what it said exactly, nor what the stuff was called, but what my wife read aloud was something like, "Brewed from random vegetation." She asked Sandy what that was supposed to mean.

"My friend Abby Greenbaum says they make it from the stuff that grows in the sidewalk cracks."

His delivery of the one-liner was charming, and I was pleased to see that my wife was moved to laugh her wonderful laugh. It boded well. She straightened her hair coquettishly, I thought.

"I stole it from Ned Brick's house after he died," he admitted to me in an aside that seemed perversely calculated to wreck the good-will he had earned thus far, but my wife's interest appeared to be absorbed in the unusual bottle.

"Should I open this?" she asked.

"Hell no," said Sandy. "Don't you have anything decent?" This earned another laugh.

"We have some red wine open, don't we, sweetie?" she said.

"I wouldn't know," said Sandy. He was on a roll!

He had pretended that my wife's "sweetie" was addressed to him, a harmless conceit that further broke the ice. We had a few drinks in the living room, and some specially spiced almonds that I handed round on a tray. He touched some of our fragile belongings in a familiar manner that made me nervous, but otherwise, everything was going along just great.

Then Sandy Baker Jr., who was wearing a denim vest, dropped an almond and it rolled under the couch.

"Chefs do this," he said. He felt around under the couch, found the dusty almond, and popped it in his mouth. I silently considered that he had just lost a few points with my wife, but then one of the cats came out and seemed to like him, though not the movie-star cat. The cat, wrong cat though it was, gave him a kiss on the elbow, which we all took as a good sign.

"He *never* does that!" my wife said, jealousy mingled with admiration in her voice. She had forgotten the dirty almond.

But when we got to the dinner table, the good times were over.

"Ugh, mushrooms," he said.

"Yes," I explained, "it's a complicated French sauce that requires cognac *and* armagnac."

"Yuck," he said.

"I'm sorry," I said.

"You worked on this all day," said my wife.

"What's for dessert?" Sandy asked.

"Chocolate mousse," I answered. "Would you like to skip right to that?"

He made a face. "Is that the world-famous treat known the world over for looking like a bad case of diarrhea?"

"I hope not," I said, rising. "I hand-whipped it."

"I bet you did," he said. "But what about the chocolate mousse?"

I cast a nervous look toward my wife. This sort of ribald talk was okay for the barroom, but not as welcome at a fancy dinner party. If my wife had caught his implication, she did not register as much.

"Nothing for you, then? That's just fine. I thought you were here to take glamour shots of my pussy anyway," she said.

I cannot guess who was more startled at the double meaning of my wife's statement—myself or Sandy Baker Jr.! The latter played it cool, of course.

"If that's what you want," he said, locking eyes with her. I have remarked before upon the uncanny power of his strange and disturbing eyes like fiendish jewels.

Nor are my wife's eyes a couple of slouches. They stared right back at him. "I thought it's what you wanted."

"Who knows what anybody wants in this crazy world?" he said. I thought it was an excellent point.

"Where's your camera?" my wife asked.

"My phone has a camera in it."

"I thought you were filling my sweetie's head with a bunch of talk about a 'special camera.'"

"It's special," he assured her. "Everything about me is special."

His cell phone didn't look special to me, but there are a lot of things I don't know about. Technology changes in the blink of an eye, causing the older among us to feel every bit our age.

Their eyes were fixed in a powerful interlocked beam of torrential psychic energy. It made me feel scared and weird, as if a couple of immortal wizards were battling for the fate of my soul.

"Your chicken is getting cold!" I shouted, hoping to startle my wife, thus breaking the mysterious spell.

It did not work.

Without tearing her eyes from his, my wife picked up a slippery piece of chicken with her fingers.

The chicken had required slow cooking for many hours. The process rendered it moist and delectable to be sure, but some of its more delicate bones had turned to slivers in the oven, I am sad to report.

A small, jagged dart of bone surprised my wife by stabbing her on the inside of the cheek. Her concentration was broken as she put her linen napkin to her mouth in the way favored by polite society in order to spit out the offending portion.

Sandy Baker Jr. laughed. "Good thing I'm skipping the chicken," he said. "I might have choked to death."

"Wouldn't that have been a shame?" my wife replied. But her zinger was interrupted by a cough and she was forced to resort to her water glass.

Sandy Baker Jr. laughed again. He had defeated her in some essential way. I was not too happy about it. It was at this point in the evening that I grabbed his bottle of strange Chicago intoxicant and began downing the vile, thick stuff with some urgency.

"I guess that's why they call it choking the chicken," he said.

His remark made little sense. At this point, I was fed up with Sandy Baker Jr. My allegiance had switched.

Of course my primary allegiance is always to my wife, but you know what I mean.

"I'm suddenly in the mood for some of your diarrhea pudding after all," said Sandy Baker Jr.

"It's chocolate mousse," I said in a surly tone.

He just laughed. You see, he knew very well it was chocolate mousse. Oh, he seemed invincible, like an evil knight.

In a way, a glimmer somewhere deep inside me admired him for his unrelenting "take charge" attitude. I went into the kitchen, opened the refrigerator, stared into its sparkling depths of awful cleanliness, and began to cry.

Here come the waterworks! mocks the reader.

Indeed. It would be wrong for me to suggest that turning your cat into a movie star is all roses and sunshine, a cakewalk, a waltz, or some other pleasurable activity. It's not just the job of making your cat into a movie star where this applies. There must come a moment when all seems lost in whatever you're doing, or you're not doing it right.

Should we take a moment to discuss St. John of the Cross and his "Dark Night of the Soul"? Probably not. But I would like to mention that it doesn't mean exactly what you think it means. I have heard the phrase "Dark Night of the Soul" misused far more often than I have heard it used correctly.

I discovered by chance that I had carried Sandy's disreputable bottle into the kitchen. I took it into the bathroom with me, locked the door and had a few slugs and sat there for quite a while, until I could make myself stop crying. My movie-star cat rustled behind the shower curtain; the bathtub was one of her favorite spots for hiding when there was a noisy stranger in the house. She had gotten herself in a funny position and couldn't quite figure out how to negotiate the curtain and escape the tub. I helped her, and it was good to take my mind off of myself for a minute.

She jumped on my lap. I gazed into her eyes, which were the color of a certain kind of shiny Greek olive you can get at a nice grocery store. She had a funny way of looking you right in the eyes.

Then she buried her face in my armpit. She thought I was her mother. I thought about how nice it was to be loved.

By the time I returned with Sandy's chocolate mousse, I was surprised to find him dancing with my wife to one of the rocking tunes I had put on my special Sandy Baker Jr. playlist.

"The chicken was great, sweetie!" my wife said. She shouted, actually, because they had turned the song way up. It turned out to be a song they both loved very much, "Strobe Light" by the B-52s. Music had brought them together, at least for the moment. In the lyrical portion, the male singer and female singer promised each other that they wanted to "make love to you under the strobe light," which rankled me in my ambivalent mood, as well as the promises from the male that he would kiss the female "on the pineapple," though clearly it was the rhythmic fun that had arrested the listeners, and after all, the selection was of my own choosing.

"I had some!" screamed Sandy, referring to the chicken. "It's okay once you pick all the mushrooms off! F***! Your wife can really dance!"

"I love to dance!" she confirmed.

"Do you guys go out dancing a lot?"

"No!"

"You should!"

"We really should! When we were first dating, we went out dancing all the time!"

If only all this merrymaking had commenced a little earlier.

The song ended. A ballad came on, Bobby Short. I was the only one who liked Bobby Short. They turned him way down. I picked at my chicken. I don't know what they were doing, just horsing around like old chums. Who was playing whom? I couldn't tell. Sometimes I think I might have a mild case of Asperger's syndrome, or a severe case of Asperger's syndrome.

"You should come hear my band."

"When?" my wife said.

"Tonight!" said Sandy Baker Jr. "I'm going to have to get on out of here pretty soon. Sound check."

"Hold it a second, hotshot," my wife said. "We haven't talked about the money yet."

"Oh."

His "oh" made it clear that he knew just what she was talking about. It was practically a confession.

"Oh!" he said again, changing his tone to something devious and jolly. "First let's get these dishes washed. You don't want to get up in the morning with a load of dirty dishes." He started collecting items to wash. I put my arm around my plate, like a man in a prison movie.

"Dishwasher's broken," said my wife. "You'll be sorry you volunteered."

"He doesn't look so broken to me. Well, maybe a little." Sandy Baker Jr. was implying that I was the dishwasher in the family. I believe it was meant to be emasculating.

"If that is meant to be an insult, I don't get it," I said. Inside I thought, What's wrong with a man washing the dishes? Nothing is wrong with a man washing the dishes.

"I like doing things the old-fashioned way!" said Sandy Baker Jr. to my wife, ignoring me.

Off they went, making little cheeping noises like little baby chickens in a chicken yard.

I guess they got the water all warm and sudsy and one washed and the other dried, and Sandy Baker Jr. was probably wearing an apron for some kind of disarming effect. Strangely attractive gloves of yellow latex were involved, I feel sure. Then my wife changed clothes and asked was I sure I didn't want to go out and hear Sandy's band.

I, on my third snifter of chocolate mousse, declined.

When my wife came home she smelled intoxicatingly of sweat, perfume, liquor, and old cigarettes. I was reclining on a chaise longue. If I may say so politely, she immediately sat athwart me and tried energetically to rekindle the old romantic spark in our marriage despite all the chocolate mousse I had inside me.

"What's got into you?" I inquired.

The cats were certainly alarmed. It may be that they had grown unaccustomed to displays quite so strenuous, mellowing as our household had with the inevitable passing of the years.

I should stop and indicate that though I enjoyed the aroma of tobacco commingled with other sins that was making my wife's skin so slick and hot, smoking is not cool, nor do I endorse it.

"What's this?" my wife asked teasingly, from atop me. She withdrew from her shirt pocket (she was wearing a white shirt with a front pocket like a man's) some twenty-dollar bills so damp and soft. There were three of them. Her pants had been shed by this point. I am not trying to be erotic, especially about my own wife. Having described her shirt, it seemed disingenuous to skip the remainder of her couture.

"I got his take of the door," she said. "It was just forty dollars, the poor dingbat. I shook another twenty out of him. I doubt we'll see any more of our money."

"Did you...*seduce* him?" I said.

"Shut up, baby," she replied.

At what I should term the highlight of our intimacy, my wife whispered into my ear, "You don't really want our cat to be a movie star, do you?"

"No," I said. "No, no."

"You would miss her too much."

"Yes!" I shouted.

"It doesn't matter, does it?" she said.

"No," I said. "It doesn't matter at all."

Marriage

"Banana cream pie. Coconut cream pie."

"Chocolate icebox pie."

"Lemon icebox pie."

"Lemon *meringue* pie."

A great deal of meaning lay in that conversation, an escalating clash, a conflict and resolution, an understanding and harmony, and none of it about pie. It is not worth explaining. You could never understand it.

Here's an easier one:

"The mail hasn't come yet."

"It hasn't come yet."

"Huh?"

"I said the mail hasn't come yet."

"Huh?"

"It hasn't come yet."

"That's what *I* said."

But perhaps most to the point:

"My stomach is upset."

"Well, you ate beans twice yesterday. Plus you are in a period of transition."

Taco Foot

Two men, Harris and Burns, met for lunch.

Harris had a baby. He brought the baby to lunch.

Burns saw Harris getting out of the Harris family minivan. Harris had to put the baby on the ground for a moment, in its little car seat. Burns walked over to say hi. In the meantime, a woman happened to be parking her car next to Harris's. Her mouth was very wide open. As if she were laughing with eagerness to kill the baby.

Harris picked up the baby in plenty of time.

It seemed to Burns, who did not have a baby, that babies were in constant and horrific danger. But he had noticed that people with babies, such as Harris, were nonchalant about it.

Harris and Burns went inside and stood in line. It was a good taco place, where you had to stand in line to order.

The cashier asked whether they were babysitting today.

Harris said that he babysat every day, by which he meant that this was his baby, and he took care of it every day.

Burns and Harris were not young men. Say their average age was forty-six. They didn't comport or groom themselves like respectable gentlemen of that age. They were unemployed. One had brown hair and one's hair was somewhat lighter than brown. They were ugly.

They poured their own sweet tea from the nozzles of big zinc urns and sat down at a table and waited for their tacos. Harris balanced the little car seat in a chair. He had to turn the chair sideways to balance the baby in its car seat properly.

Burns said to Harris, in reference to the curious cashier, "I should have told her the baby has two daddies. That would have been funny."

The tacos came and the men began to eat the tacos.

The baby put its foot in its mouth.

"Look at that," said Burns. "Your baby thinks its foot is a taco."

"Her foot," said Harris.

"What?" said Burns. Then Burns said to the baby, "Well, well, well. Do you think your foot is a taco? I'm going to call you Taco Foot."

Burns said to Harris, "From now on I'm going to call your baby Taco Foot. You should put a little soft taco shell on your baby's foot. Old Taco Foot. You should dress up your baby like a taco for Halloween. That would make a good costume. You should decorate old Taco Foot with lettuce and tomato. Isn't that right, Taco Foot?"

"I'm getting sick of you," said Harris.

"When you've wasted your life, part of you is like, 'Gosh, that's terrible.' And part of you is like, 'Oh well. I guess I should have thought of this sooner,'" said Burns.

"You probably haven't wasted your life," said Harris.

"You had a baby," said Burns. "That's supposed to be a pretty good setup by all accounts."

"It's not bad," said Harris.

"Let me be frank," said Burns. "I asked you to lunch today because I'm in love with your wife."

"When did this happen?" said Harris. "I ought to take this bottle of hot sauce and pour it in your eyes."

Was Harris joking? It was hard to tell.

Burns wasn't joking.

"Don't get me wrong," said Burns. "I'm not going to tell her. I'm never going to tell her. I'm going to walk around with a broken heart."

"Congratulations," said Harris.

"Once she was nursing old Taco Foot at a party and I didn't even realize it. I was just standing there talking to her. And then Taco Foot's head slid off, didn't it, Taco Foot? I saw everything. Marcie looked all red and ruddy, like she had been out in the sun."

"Marcie's tits are not red," said Harris.

"Healthful," said Burns. "They had a healthful look to them. Don't use such crude language in reference to your incredible wife."

"I'm going to kill you," said Harris.

"Well, I'll see you later," said Burns. He wiped his mouth on a napkin. "Sorry to spring this on you. Now I feel awkward."

Burns was sitting at a red light when the minivan attacked him. Harris was bumping Burns's little car from behind, trying to push him into oncoming traffic. Burns looked in the rearview mirror and saw Harris's mad face but not Taco Foot, who was probably strapped safely into place.

Burns answered his phone.

"You twat," said Harris's voice. "This is what you get."

"We can't be punished for our thoughts," said Burns.

"Oh yes we can," said Harris.

Tornado

WHEN JAMES DROVE HIS CAR INTO THE TORNADO, HE THOUGHT OF the huge window with French shutters by their bed. In the morning, when they undid the shutters, there stood the biggest camellia bush they'd ever seen growing out of control, it almost filled the whole window, squashed up against the glass like an eager beast. The haunted camellia bush. The witch's fingers. They said a lot of silly things back then. Whenever they'd get a big storm or a strong wind the camellia would make a clawing noise at night against the window—a horrible, squeaky clawing sound, which, as he drove helplessly into the tornado, he remembered in perfect detail.

He remembered asking her whether they had a can of that Italian wedding soup he liked. She said, "Look in the cabinet." He said, "I'm too tired to look in the cabinet." One time she said, "I don't want to talk about the things that haunt me." And he was like, "Good. Jesus! Let's don't." Looking back on it, maybe she *had* wanted to talk about the things that haunted her.

.

Detective

"How much do you charge?" Granger said.

"For what?" she said.

"To follow a guy."

"What kind of guy?"

"A guy like Cowboy Bob."

"What's the angle?"

"I just want to know everything he does, everything he says."

"Oh, is that all?"

"See, I stopped doing things at some point. I don't do things. In writing, the preference is for characters who do things. I want to turn Cowboy Bob into a character. As a character, Cowboy Bob will appeal to a certain demographic. In particular, I trust, the distaff side, who form a much more active readership than their male counterparts, according to respected surveys."

"You want me to follow somebody around so you can make pages out of him. That the gist?"

"Sure. You provide the raw material of a life, I fashion it into art. In addition to your fee, I'll thank you in the acknowledgments section."

"What about Cowboy Bob? You plan on thanking him? In your little acknowledgments section?"

"That doesn't seem wise. This would be strictly between us. You and me. A professional arrangement. I assume you have some sort of confidentiality clause in your contract?"

"I'm no rat, if that's what you're asking."

"By the way, my last acknowledgements section wasn't 'little.' It was over thirty pages long. I'm thorough, and I think you'll find I'm grateful in a perceptive and extremely flattering way."

"So you're going to basically take this guy's life without his permission and crap all over it."

"Oh, he'd never know. Not in a million years. See, by the time it hits the page…see, what we writers do is…well, I don't know. I don't have any idea."

"You spin straw into gold."

"That's it."

"Some poor schmuck should feel lucky to be immortalized by you."

"Well, he wouldn't know, but sure. The great part is, it works equally well if his glamorous bad-boy persona is all a sham and he spends his free time reading *The Bridges of Madison County* out loud to his comatose grandmother. I want to get that straight right up front. You don't have to worry if the material doesn't seem exciting enough to you. That's where the power of fiction comes in."

"I spent some of my childhood near Portland, Oregon. My grandmother made pickles in the washing machine."

"Uh-huh."

"So is that yours now? That part of my life?"

"It's already filed away up here."

"I want to be my granny. That's my goal."

"You want to make pickles in the washing machine?"

"I don't have a washing machine."

"You could do it at the laundromat."

"You know, I've always wanted to dye clothes at the laundro-mat. But I don't have the balls."

"I find that hard to believe."

"How do I know you're not a weirdo?" she asked.

Granger didn't answer. He *was* a weirdo!

Dazzling Ladies of Science Fiction

THEY GOT DOWN TO THE BUSINESS OF DICE. PUFFER AND BRICK TOOK most of Laurel's money. They tried to be nice and let her win some back, but she didn't want their charity.

Hurt couldn't focus on the game, which was called ace-four twenty-four and played with a worn leather cup. He had watched the men playing it at the bar on multiple occasions, but it remained obscure to him. His mind went away. He thought about writing on the bar napkin but recalled the look that Brick had given him over that habit in the past. And rightfully so. There was something trashy about trying to capture other people on a napkin, or on any kind of paper. Sometimes he was experimenting, writing little stories that would fit on a napkin. But most of the time he was a jackal, stealing people's biz. "Very fly," Laurel had said about something, and it seemed sweetly antiquated. He had to jot it down.

While the rest of them played dice at the bar, Hurt tried to stop doodling the blurbs he thought he might get ("Sweeping") and concentrate on the holes in the outline of his multigenerational domestic literary novel. What had really happened to Mr. Timberlake's late wife? Hurt had assumed a lingering cancer. But what if the son, Skunk, were to blame for his mother's death? That was always a winner. Forgot his humble place as a craftsman of pie catalogs, became ambitious, tragically so, wrote about his mother on a napkin. And what, suicide? That earnest cliché?

Hurt remembered some women's butts he had seen on TV. Why? There had been a suicide on the show. His brain was trying to tell him something.

They were characters on a space show and whenever they went marching up the ramp into their spaceship you could see their butts.

Their pants were tight but gave the impression of being sturdy, accurate, and functional, as though the special-effects team had researched them. You thought, yes, those are what space pants will really look like in the future, made of silver car upholstery. These pants are necessary for their well-being and survival in the subzero wastes of outer space. It is a coincidence how you can see the outlines of their butts.

It was a universal joy, looking at the butts of hot ladies in spacesuits. People had been doing it since the dawn of entertainment.

Hurt got the notion that Skunk's mother had been a calendar model in the late 1960s, a pinup in astronaut gear, cocking a big ray gun against a cheesy, wrinkled backdrop of the moon. A calendar called *Hot Ladies of Outer Space*. No, *Hot Ladies of Science Fiction*. It could be a book title, one of those book titles that promises something other than what the book delivers to teach readers a valuable lesson. Hurt could be one of those dudes who goes slumming in genre fiction to universal acclaim.

Interesting to have a fat loser like Skunk, who probably spends all his time on the computer looking up images of hot ladies in spacesuits with the "safe search" option turned off, discover that his revered mother had been one of those very ladies.

When did "hot" become a synonym for "sexy"? Every word he ever chose reminded him of how much he didn't know and was too tired to find out. *Sexy Ladies of Science Fiction.*

His pen was poised, doing nothing over the napkin. Hurt wasn't going to remember any of this when he got home.

Dazzling Ladies of Science Fiction. Would have sounded classier, more respectable to the ears of the time.

It was a problem, marrying a leggy international beauty to a meek little priss like Mr. Timberlake. Or was it kind of perfect?

Mr. Timberlake lived in Hurt's house, and by extension in a town like Hurt's town. There would be a chemical plant slowly poisoning the surrounding areas: huge pipes through which they blast a scent like magnolia that covers the town and makes everyone feel relaxed. It's to cover up the acrid stench of fatal chemicals.

It would be a perfect place for the *Dazzling Ladies of Science Fiction* calendar tour. The headquarters of the chemical company are in Rome. The Italian chemical company is one of the sponsors of the calendar—*the* sponsor. They are sending the Dazzling Ladies of Science Fiction on a tour of all their chemical plants for publicity. Hurt's novel would span the globe. "A globe-spanning tour de force," he jotted.

What kind of job would a gentleman like Mr. Timberlake have at a chemical plant?

He might have been a research chemist who now in his retirement maintains a small personal laboratory in a back shed. There he creates the most refined soaps the world has ever known and gives them out on special occasions. He never sells them.

Mr. Timberlake has a superior sense of smell. This gives him a reason to sit in his dilapidated lawn chair, soaking his feet, staring at nothing, smelling all the many smells of nature in their many combinations, smells so subtle that no one else can discern them, and he translates them into soaps that the layman can enjoy—soaps that hint at the smells only Mr. Timberlake can smell, soaps that repre- sent the nearest we will ever come to experiencing the world through

Mr. Timberlake's extraordinary nose. He considers everything to be nature, including diesel fumes. His ideas are so advanced that he seems like a crackpot to many, including his resentful and belittling son Skunk.

What does it say about the relationship that Mr. Timberlake has given his son such a nickname? Or that Skunk has given it to himself, in defiance?

The soaps of Mr. Timberlake are ethereal. They dissolve like the skirls of foam on the shore.

What was a skirl?

Look up skirls when you get home, Hurt.

Everybody Hurt knew had a nice phone, the kind you could sit in a bar like this and look up skirls on.

Not Hurt.

Hurt had a bar napkin. Hurt had bupkis.

Bar napkins were supposed to make you feel like Hemingway or Picasso.

The soaps of Mr. Timberlake can barely withstand a single dampening. It's like washing your hands with a frigging moonbeam.

Skunk spends all his time losing money on internet gambling. Some bad men come to him.

Your father's recipes are worth a fortune. We want to analyze them so we can make the soaps last longer. (This is strictly against Mr. Timberlake's elegantly expressed philosophy of soaps.)

All Skunk has to do is distract his father while the bad men use bolt cutters on the shed door.

But then something goes horribly wrong. So the dust jacket would say.

Hurt felt that this version of Mr. Timberlake was becoming too brilliant and grandiose. Mr. Timberlake was no wizard. And who was that lousy son of King Arthur? The one in black armor? That wasn't

Skunk, no sir. Skunk didn't have the black metallic heart of a usurper. Mordred.

Forget the magical soap that makes your dreams come true. It put Hurt in mind of that awful movie where Dustin Hoffman was a benevolent gnome who owned a shop where all the toys came to life.

Dustin Hoffman would be great as Mr. Timberlake in the movie version, though. "Hoffman returns to form in this sure-to-be-timeless classic."

He wrote MALE SECRETARY on the napkin and everyone was too busy shooting dice to notice. Hurt tried to remember why he shouldn't be writing on the napkin, which brought him back to his original idea. How had Skunk inadvertently caused his mother's death by writing on a napkin?

There was the tontine angle. Hurt had wanted to write about a tontine ever since he had encountered the concept on an episode of *The Simpsons* in 1996.

Forty years ago, all twelve Dazzling Ladies of Science Fiction made an appearance in the lobby of a swank Miami hotel. They laughingly hid an antique brooch under a three-foot-tall cylindrical ashtray filled with immaculate sand. The last surviving DLOSF will come back and claim it.

Now all of them are gone except Sally Silver and her best friend, her friend who never left the business, her rich and glamorous friend who lives high on the hog as the hostess of a literary salon and occasionally plays faded old beauties in somber independent dramas about Alzheimer's disease. If Sally Silver hadn't ditched it all for Mr. Timberlake, this might have been her life! But she is not jealous. It has been so long since she has seen her old friend. A trip to Miami will be just the thing to revive both of their spirits, for of course the old movie star with all her attainments and glory has secret troubles of her own.

Skunk volunteers to chauffer. When they reach the old movie star's house (she lives somewhere on the way to Miami, wherever rich people have country estates between Mississippi and Miami) they get a surprise: a third Dazzling Lady is still alive after all—a tart-tongued old alky who was Sally Silver's sworn enemy in the olden days. Now she's a sassy granny who wears mascara and tells it like it is!

A terrible car crash on the way to pick up the object of the tontine. It is Skunk's fault. He has been writing about his mother on a napkin. She is offended and Skunk is banned from the car. So he leaves her. Or she leaves him. They part. She takes over. But she's too old and blind to drive.

If Skunk hadn't written on that napkin, he would have been driving, and his mother would be alive today, etc.

What about the napkin is so offensive?

What would this woman—whose model name was Sally Silver—find offensive?

Before we can know, she needs a history.

She needs to give up the life of an international model for Mr. Timberlake.

Why?

Mr. Timberlake does something gallant that attracts her attention. He takes up for her. He is presented as a contrast to her avaricious manager.

They run away to a neighboring county and are married by a justice of the peace. It is a purely romantic impulse.

What is the history of the woman whose actions we have described?

A farm girl from Kansas, whisked away by the jet set, having lost touch with her rustic roots, temporarily mad for the horses and cows, the barns and bales she sees through the windows of her limousine.

Does she place all her affection for her past into the person of this courtly, even virginal man who does her a kindness?

Wouldn't she come to regret it?

Hurt didn't want to make either of them unsympathetic. They are devoted to one another, yet heroically unsuited.

She starts her own business from the home, designing and hand-sewing a line of science fiction–themed headbands.

She has a hot, sloppy affair with the town's bachelor farmer, a gentle giant based on old Puffer over here, whatever his real name was. Hurt had never caught it.

One night, the night after Skunk has been banned from the car, they are driving through a mist, a silvery mist. And they come upon a hitchhiker, their old friend Olivia, standing weirdly beside a deserted country road in the silver mist, wearing the silver slacks that made her butt so famous, the silver jumpsuit, her beehive hair as it looked on her TV show, except now it has turned silver. Otherwise she looks strangely young. She is a beautiful old African-American woman with limpid eyes. Hurt was clearly seeing the woman who had played Uhura in the original *Star Trek* series. He couldn't stop himself, she appeared out of the mist.

Of course, the silver pantsuit was his own invention. Well, he had stolen it from that other TV show. But if not for his magnificent, writerly brain making connections…

He was too fond of the word *silver*.

We hear about Olivia only from inconclusive e-mails and phone messages sent from the road. She never speaks, she never eats, she just rides with them, a harbinger of something. She is solid enough. The other women prod and pinch her. Skunk and Mr. Timberlake have a hard time piecing together this information. Isn't Olivia dead? Didn't she die? Everyone seems to vaguely recall hearing that Olivia had died at some point.

When they get to the hotel, it's not there. It burned down in the 1980s. Maybe Olivia walks into the space where the hotel used to be and disappears.

It would be nice if the burned-out old hull of the hotel was still standing, but would that be realistic?

Skunk knew about the fire.

Here lies the heart of his culpability.

He knew the trip would end in blackened timbers, that the past had vanished and could not be reproduced or recaptured, no matter what that old gasbag Faulkner said. It was the prefab tragic ending of Skunk's story, which he was writing for a national magazine. A human-interest piece that would elevate him from the world of pie catalogs forever. Skunk was, like Truman Capote as depicted in motion pictures, pushing reality, nudging it toward a desirable outcome for his article. Only his mother didn't cotton to being used as human interest, especially without her knowledge, especially by her own son. And now to discover that he was willingly driving them forward into heartbreak!

Upon discovering the ruination and emptiness of life, the old women are destroyed. Their oldness comes out. Olivia—representing their glory or something—has melted and merged with the ashes and now they are just three tired, sick old women on the highway. Thus depleted of their essences thanks to Skunk's machinations, and speeding along in the wee hours of the night because they wish to put as much distance as possible between them and the site of their mortal dreams, one of them falls asleep at the wheel—it has to be her, it has to be Skunk's mother, and he must be haunted by the question of whether she fell asleep at the wheel or did it on purpose—and they drive under a rumbling log truck, and the Dazzling Ladies of Science Fiction are no more.

Part of Hurt knew that this all had to do with his pending divorce. How he got from there to matricide was not something he wanted to consider. If you thought about such things too much you couldn't write.

MALE SECRETARY looked charming on the napkin. A pedestrian job for Mr. Timberlake, but one of deep attentiveness and servitude, like that sad butler in the book about the sad butler.

Mr. Timberlake is like the sad butler who could only cry on the inside!

In the book, people would always be trying to "help" him "reclaim" his "dignity" by saying "personal assistant" or "executive assistant," and Mr. Timberlake would proudly insist on his respectable station as a male secretary of the highest order and would never let anyone get away with trying to gussy it up in newfangled lingo as if it were a secret shame.

Why was Mr. Timberlake Skunk's father? Why wasn't Skunk's father more like Hurt's father?

Hurt's father was an agile and boisterous man, unlike Mr. Timberlake in every way.

And why was Skunk's mother dead? What would Hurt's mother make of that?

When was the last time Hurt had visited his parents?

What about Hurt's brother, who lived so far away?

What about Hurt's sister?

In your last novel you gave the characters your parents' names. You think if you amass and collate a sufficient amount of superficial details—how stiff the legs of your father's pants got after a week on the shrimp boat, how he picked the trash fish out of the nets, how after a while he would see the sun on the horizon and not know whether it was coming up or going down, about the swells so high nothing could be cooked on the stovetop—a true portrait will emerge.

What you end up with is just fiction.

Appendix:
Hurt's Napkin Stories

Wheelbarrow

Hired a young couple to push me around in my wheelbarrow. They're not a couple, but I'd like to see them get together. I'd like to fix them up. Maybe they'll bond over how much they hate pushing me around in my wheelbarrow.

Texaco Sign

Travelers say that all of Oklahoma is covered in a white fog. The only thing visible is a tall Texaco sign, and beneath it three enormous white plastic tiles with red letters that spell out EAT.

Maybe when you get there it's a plate of chicken, or maybe the sign keeps receding and receding and you never find out what there is to eat.

One report has come back: a coyote chasing a little white dog, but the sighting cannot be confirmed and it may have been an illusion brought on by the fog.

Encouragement

I think about all the encouragement I've received over the years. Are people just being friendly? Or do they hate me?

Mississippi River

I'll never forget the first time Bill saw the Mississippi River.
He said, "Who cares?"

The Black Parasol

AMY O'BRIEN, ALL ALONE, TOOK A WALK AT NIGHT THROUGH THE dilapidated town square of Ordain, Mississippi, to the creepy old doll hospital where the horrible murders had taken place. She pressed her palm to the cool lemon stucco just as lightning struck.

O'Brien ducked around the corner and under an awning. Big, slow drops of rain began to pelt the canvas.

Past the end of the alley was a bar she had never noticed, made of red cinder blocks. It had a glossy black wooden door. Warm yellow light streamed from the dirty windows.

The rain and wind picked up. She ran for it.

The insides were dimmer and gloomier than the welcoming light had suggested. At the end of the long bar, one old man shook dice in a long leather cup while another old man watched. A jowly, furtive middle-aged couple sat at a table in a far corner, staring at their empty glasses.

The rain came harder still. The bar's corrugated tin roof rang and roared with it, a sound both pleasant and frightening.

O'Brien stood just inside the door. There was no bartender. Powerful rumbling rattled the bottles. She stepped up bravely and took her place on a stool. O'Brien steadied herself, putting her hands on the clammy bar. The surface was light green streaked with black, made of futuristic material, like a kitchen counter from the 1950s, so ugly. The old men kept going with their game. O'Brien turned and tried to get a better look at the soft, chubby couple—man and wife, she imagined, having a terrible anniversary.

When she turned again the bartender was there, slicing up a puny lime on a white plastic cutting board as if he'd been there the whole time. He looked up at her and smiled. He was a handsome, dark guy with crooked teeth and a funny hat. Like, a half black guy, maybe? Not that it mattered. She kicked herself for even wondering. The air smelled like limes. O'Brien heard guitar music, snatches and hints above the rain outside.

"You ordering, sweetheart?" said the bartender.

"Yes, please."

He wiped his hands on his apron.

"Got some ID on you, sweetheart?"

"Oh, I'm twenty-five. I get that a lot."

"Still need to see it, darling."

He didn't look any older than O'Brien, and certainly not old enough to call women "sweetheart" and "darling" with such casual sincerity. Was it some irritating Mississippi affectation? She thought she would say something about it, but didn't. She gave him her driver's license.

"Could I get a white wine spritzer?"

He laughed at her.

"Something funny?"

"It's a funny drink."

"Yeah, I know," she said. "Yeah, but it's what I want."

"You got it, sweetheart."

The bottle of white he grabbed from the little glass-doored cooler had about a quarter left in it, the cork barely jammed into the neck.

She finished half her drink in two desperate gulps.

"Oh baby," she said.

"Whoa, you really wanted that white wine spritzer."

"Brother, you have no idea. Tell me about your hat."

He took it off and examined it. His hair was very curly. He frowned and picked a piece of lint off the crown of his funny hat.

"Want to hold it?" he said.

"No thanks, sport."

He showed it to her from a number of angles. "It's felt, but sturdy. It's bespoke. Do you know what that means?"

"Yes."

"Okay, a lot of people don't know what that means. But okay, you're all right. I dated this hatter from Tennessee. She's famous on the internet. I did a lot of research on this hat." He put it on again, cocked it just so. "Some call it a Goober hat or a Jughead hat. I saw an old picture of one and they called it a whoopee cap. It was also associated with juvenile delinquency. You're supposed to stick collectible pins in it, but I don't choose to do that. The felt is mulberry, an unusual color for this kind of hat. My girlfriend picked it out, my ex-girlfriend, the well-known hatter, she picked out the color, said it went well with my rich skin tone. Well, you'd have to see it in the light."

O'Brien downed the rest of her spritzer. "That was one sour-ass spritzer," she said.

"Yeah, I'm sorry, honey. Don't serve much white wine in here. I'm sure that bottle was pretty skunky. Want the rest of it? No charge."

"Hell yes," she said.

The door blew open. A flash of purple lightning showed a tall, thin figure draped in a long black cape. O'Brien could smell stinking wet wool all the way across the room.

"No book tonight, Doctor?"

The cadaverous stranger shook his head.

"Too wet, I guess," said the bartender.

The man hung his dripping cape on a peg by the door. His slate-dark hair, parted in the middle, reached his shoulders. Putting down his twisty walking stick, he wrung out one side of his hair and then the other, splashing rainwater on the floor, and moved to a large round table in the middle of the bar, obviously his regular spot.

The bartender got a cheap bottle of port and filled a whole water glass with it. After he had delivered it to the tall, thin man, he came back and leaned over the bar, speaking quietly to O'Brien as if in confidence. "Dr. Cherubino. He usually brings his big black book. It must be two feet tall and a foot across and five inches thick. I don't know how he carries it. He lays it out on that table there and gets out an old ink bottle and some blotting paper and writes in it with a big old goose-quill pen."

"What is it?"

"You should go ask him about it."

O'Brien looked over her shoulder. The man was there in the dark, staring at her. She gave a little shudder.

"No thanks."

The bartender pushed another spritzer in front of her.

"How old you think he is?"

O'Brien took the tiniest sip of the new spritzer. She grimaced.

"Oh, that's the worst," she said. "Yeah, I don't want to look at him again. I don't know, fifty-five?"

"That's the thing. He must be eighty. He's been all over the world. People gave him herbs and all kinds of things to make him live longer. Techniques and secrets."

Despite herself, O'Brien looked back at the doctor again. He was crumbling something into his port, maybe a dried leaf.

"You should talk to him. What else are you going to do? You two would really hit it off."

"Seems like a loner."

"Aw, he's an old ham."

The bartender went back to his sad lime. O'Brien contemplated her flat spritzer. She looked back at the old man and thought what the hell. She went over.

"Hi, I'm O'Brien. Do you mind if I sit down?"

He spoke without looking at her. "When I was a young man I broke my back entirely. I was healed by a weird shaman."

O'Brien took it as a yes. She pulled out a chair at the end of the table.

"I like your stick," she said.

"Crepe myrtle," he said. And now that she was seated he looked at her. "According to Robert Graves, the myrtle is simultaneously the tree of love and the tree of death."

"Wow," said O'Brien.

Dr. Cherubino's face was drawn and sunken, streaked with violet but not especially wrinkled. His eyes glowed black.

"What about this book of yours?" said O'Brien. "I'm hearing about a book."

Dr. Cherubino looked down at the table as if expecting to see his book in its usual place.

"I collect ghost stories," he said. "Ghosts interest us because they seem to blur so many lines we don't acknowledge—and by blurring, to make them clearer, curiously. Presence and absence, life and death, dreaming and waking, the real and the unreal, sanity and madness. These are just a few of the categories we refer to as 'opposites,' unthinkingly."

"So you write ghost stories?"

"I seek them out. I try to record them faithfully. Do you have any?"

"Who, me? No. I mean, I apparently said some strange things as a kid."

"Please elaborate."

"You know, I'm Korean. I don't know if that has anything to do with it. Don't ever remember being there. I was adopted, obvi. I complained that somebody named 'Hot Dog' was keeping me up all night making faces at me, which everybody thought was hilarious. And Mom said, 'Are they funny faces?' Apparently I shook really hard, I shook all over, and I said, 'No, he scare me.' Wow, I had forgotten. It's stupid. 'He scare me.'" She laughed. "Creepy."

"I'd like more details, if you please," said Dr. Cherubino.

O'Brien shrugged. "I was little. There was other stuff."

"If I might interview your parents…"

"They don't remember it any better than I do, really. It's just things we say when we get together. I don't know if you can even call them memories anymore. Just silly things we say that make us laugh. Inside jokes, family stuff."

The bartender approached. "I'm stepping outside for a smoke," he said. "Y'all need anything?"

"I'd be honored to buy you a drink," said Dr. Cherubino to O'Brien. "I hope you will be encouraged to continue our conversation over it."

"Maybe just a bitters and soda," she said. "But you don't have to pay."

"Bitters and soda on the house, sweetheart," said the bartender. He went to get it.

"I don't believe I know your people," said Dr. Cherubino. He took a luxurious swallow of bad port and licked his lips. "Are they immigrants to the area?"

"This area?" said O'Brien. "I'm not from around here."

Dr. Cherubino looked disappointed. He dabbed at himself with a cocktail napkin. "My work is exclusively concerned with a fifty-mile radius, of which I like to fancy this establishment the exact center," he said.

He leaned in. O'Brien leaned back. He leaned in closer, his hot breath like an expensive and dreadful cheese. O'Brien moved her chair.

"Are you quite aware," he said.

"Bitters and soda," the bartender interrupted, bringing the drink.

"Pretty," said O'Brien.

It *was* pretty—a big, clean water glass. There were bubbles and lots of ice. The angostura wafted pinkly, coloring the water.

"I put a lime in it," said the bartender. He looked proud.

O'Brien turned and looked at his butt as he walked away, apron strings tied above it. He had a little spring in his step. He pushed his bespoke hat forward on his head in what he probably thought of as "a jaunty angle."

When she turned back to face the doctor, his big, sad eyes looked like hypno wheels. His long hair hung down, the color of a gravestone rubbing with a No. 2 pencil. He was an uncanny-looking dude wearing a lot of rings with gems of dark colors, blood and indigo. His caved-in cheeks were like black holes trying to suck in the rest of his face. He should have had moss growing on him. His eyelashes were like cobwebs.

"My dear, you look peaked," he said. "A sip of soda might do you good."

She looked at it, paranoid. Sure it was pretty. It glowed, like a witch's frosted house. Drink it down. The magic potion. Come on, dearie, it's just like medicine. Where was she? She didn't know anybody. Dr. Cherubino and the bartender could be in on it together. They could be adept at luring.

"As I was saying before we were interrupted, you find yourself in the most haunted area of the United States, as far as such things can be measured. Much of the evidence is anecdotal, inevitably."

"That's so interesting, listen, I'm going to be going," said O'Brien as she rose.

"Oh, my dear," said Dr. Cherubino. He grabbed his walking stick, which was leaned against the table, and hoisted himself up an inch or two—out of politeness, maybe.

The bartender came through the front door, through which he had supposedly gone for a smoke, and strode toward the table with alarming speed, an unlit cigarette behind his ear.

"This is it," O'Brien said out loud. Her legs shook.

"I'm sorry," the bartender said when he reached the table. "I've just got to try that, if you don't mind."

"Uh, sure," said O'Brien.

He downed her bitters and soda, over half the glass, and grinned with his pretty, crooked teeth. It really made him happy.

"I'm sorry, darling. I couldn't get my mind off of it. It just looked so doggone tasty. I'm going to put it on the menu. I'm going to name it after you. I'll make you another one. I'll make you another O'Brien."

"That was bizarrely presumptuous," she said, but she was smiling. "No, I'm okay, I think."

The bartender flopped into the empty chair between O'Brien and Dr. Cherubino with some force.

"Yeah, it's dead in this dump," he said. "Let's move this party somewhere happening."

"The young lady and I have business," said Dr. Cherubino.

"What kind of business?"

"Business that is none of yours."

"Ouch," said the bartender.

O'Brien laughed. "I think he wants to put me in his book," she said.

"See, now, that's an honor," said the bartender. "I'm not in your book. Am I? Why am I not in your book? I've been around a lot longer than she has. I have a cousin who's done all kinds of stuff. She threw up a demon. Hey, I should get some credit. I'm the one who told her about your book."

"It is emphatically not your place to publicize the personal interests or avocations of your customers."

"You're probably right," said the bartender. "But you do carry a pretty damn big book everywhere you go. Not like it's a secret."

"We should continue our interview at my home, away from prying ears and eyes," said Dr. Cherubino to O'Brien. "The rain seems to have stopped, and the walk will be pleasant in its aftermath. You can see the book resting on its special podium. I'll take a few notes, nothing obtrusive, it will be much the same as passing the time in genial conversation. I have some excellent imported cheese of peculiar quality you might be interested in sampling for your pleasure."

"I don't know about wandering off. I don't know my way around very well, not just yet."

"But I'll guide you, my dear. A leisurely walking tour. There are several haunted spots of some note betwixt here and there. I'd adore to gauge your elemental reaction."

"I don't know. I don't think I'd like to walk home alone past, um…"

"Revenants?" said Dr. Cherubino.

"Sure," said O'Brien.

"I'll take you over there," said the bartender, "and get you home safe, too. Where did you say you're staying?"

"I didn't," said O'Brien.

"Have you ever been to my home, young man?" Dr. Cherubino asked the bartender. "I do not think you have ever been invited. In fact, I should be alarmed to discover that such was the case."

"I know where it is. People point to it when they drive by. It's an area of local interest."

"I don't suppose it is you who tosses his losing lottery tickets into my bushes," said Dr. Cherubino.

"Boys, boys, there's no need to fight over little old me," O'Brien said. She laughed. Dr. Cherubino and the bartender looked genuinely puzzled. She frowned at them.

"I do understand the desire for a chaperone," said Dr. Cherubino. "In fact, I commend it."

"Oh, yeah," said the bartender. "Me and her? We're old buddies. I'm like her big brother basically. Right, sis?"

He reached over to put his hand on her shoulder and O'Brien jerked it away. The bartender laughed. He stood up and yelled at the old men rolling dice on the bar. "Gentlemen, I hate to break it to you but gambling is illegal!"

This got an appreciative reaction from the old-timers. The stouter of the two, the one who wore overalls, scooped up most of the pile of dollar bills, leaving some of them behind for the bartender. His unhappy, sallow friend wore a shiny old suit. With a shaky hand he plucked his fedora from the bar and put it on. His friend in overalls helped him off the stool.

"Guess that does it," the bartender said when the old men finally made it out the door. "It's deader than hell tonight. What do you say let's shut this sucker down? Won't take me two seconds. I got it down to a science."

"What about that couple in the back? Their glasses were already empty when I got here."

"What couple in the back?" said the bartender.

There was no couple in the back.

While the bartender was closing up, O'Brien walked out front. The summer storm was over. She called her boyfriend. He didn't answer. He was at the Hialeah racetrack in Florida, shooting an ironic serial killer movie. He never answered. So she texted him that she was going to an unknown location with two strange men.

AVENGE ME, she texted.

When the bartender emerged, he took the tarpaulin off of his motorcycle and sidecar. He felt the seat of the sidecar to make sure it was dry for O'Brien. He gave her a helmet, much too large.

It didn't take long to get to the doctor's house, and O'Brien was disappointed because she enjoyed the ride, pushing the big helmet around on her head to watch the stars come out where the sky had cleared, smelling grass and ozone, noticing the black leaves of the trees wetly sparkling.

As remote as the town was, though, it *was* a town. There were occasional sidewalks. It wasn't the way she and her boyfriend had imagined. The doctor's neighborhood could have been any quiet neighborhood—say a Polish neighborhood in Toronto.

They stopped in front of the doctor's cozy-looking little house.

The bartender disembarked. He removed his helmet, retrieved his funny hat from the compartment where he kept it, and put it on very carefully. Only then did he help O'Brien out of the sidecar.

"That was a blast," she said.

"Don't take much to make you happy," he said.

His hand remained on her arm.

"I'm having an adventure," she said.

"House is dark. Did he say he was walking?" He left her in the yard, sprinted up the walkway, and rang the doorbell. He cupped his hands next to his eyes and tried to look in. "I think I hear somebody bumping around in there."

"Here he comes," said O'Brien.

Streetlights were few, but the gaunt bird took the middle of the empty street, wings of his cloak fluttering behind him.

"We can't get in the front way," he said. "My apologies. The screen door is permanently stuck."

He took them around the house, up the back steps, and through a small screened-in porch, perfectly square and cluttered. He let them into a tidy kitchen which had the faint but unpleasant scent of vinegar, possibly used as a cleaning agent.

The doctor placed his cane in an umbrella stand and hung his cape over it so that it resembled a dingy ghost.

He said, "I promised you cheese."

They watched as he removed a pale wedge from his refrigerator, watched as he shuffled with it to the counter, where he carefully removed each of his rings and lined them up in a particular order before choosing a utensil from a wooden knife block.

He got out a sheet of wax paper, smoothed it on the counter, unwrapped the cheese, and set to work cutting it, wincing once as the tip of the knife entered his thumb.

He held a blood-speckled cube of whitish cheese to the light and frowned.

"Bad augury," he said.

"Uh-oh," said the bartender.

Dr. Cherubino put his thumb in his mouth and sucked thoughtfully.

Once he had cheese and crackers lying on a plate, Dr. Cherubino returned his rings to his fingers and had O'Brien and the bartender follow him down a dark hallway toward the front room.

The narrow hall was made narrower by bookcases on each side. The bookcases were full. Books were piled on top of many of them, and stacks of books sat on the floor against the wall wherever there was space. Above the bookcases there appeared to be old prints or etchings, though it was too dark to tell what they were. The air was thick with the sweet rot of paper. O'Brien sneezed three times, rapidly.

"Bless you, bless you, bless you," said Dr. Cherubino.

They came into a large, scantly furnished room with an expensive-looking rug on the wooden floor and a podium set up as if for an audience of two, for it faced a loveseat, the room's only place to sit. Hanging on the walls in bulky, chipped frames were torn old photographs of wildly bearded men with glittering expressions and sternly coiffed women who seemed to have peach pits where their eyes should have been.

At a distance behind the podium were two closed French doors with blue velvet drapes hanging inside them and hiding the next room from view.

"The haunted sewing room," Dr. Cherubino said, gesturing at the closed doors. "I do not own a coffee table. If you don't mind, we'll place your refreshments on the ottoman."

O'Brien and the bartender sat on the mahogany loveseat, which was cushioned in stripes of purple velvet—dark and lighter purple alternately. They were close by necessity, facing Dr. Cherubino's maple podium, carved on which was the motto *IN ARENA AEDIFICAS*. Another large room behind the guests—an open dining room, unlighted—made the hair on the backs of their necks stand up. They could feel it behind them, and both were compelled to turn their heads and look into the dark for a moment. It contained a table and chairs, a Victrola, and as far as they could tell, nothing else.

Purplish beams from a streetlight striped the room. Dr. Cherubino lit several large black candles—on the mantel, a small table, and the windowsills—to help.

O'Brien and the bartender stared at him with some anticipation as he solemnly took his place behind the podium and opened the ponderous book with a creak and a great thud.

"Herein I have recorded, largely from eyewitness accounts, tales of untimely visitations from the phantom realms and other unusual occurrences. Amnesia, holy smells, stigmata, somnambulism—"

"Holy smells?" said O'Brien.

"Intimates of the Catholic saint Padre Pio could smell him when he wasn't there. The false messiah Sabattai Sevi was said to exude a marvelous aroma, so much so that the peasants began to gossip that he was using perfume. Naturally, neither of these fascinating mystics falls under the scope of my humble study. I bring them up merely as notable examples from human history. Locally, I have an interesting case involving hand lotion. But I think that to laymen such as yourselves, even a gifted one such as Miss O'Brien, an old-fashioned ghost story would be most pleasurable, most free of dry and pedantic speculations. There are several from which to choose."

"What's the scariest one you've got?" said the bartender.

"I would say without hesitation that the most chilling example I have collected to date is the story I call 'The Black Parasol.'"

"Tell us that one, then."

"I cannot. It is too chilling."

"I think I can handle it," said O'Brien. "Does the spirit of 'Silky' Dick Smythe haunt the abandoned doll hospital?"

Dr. Cherubino looked displeased. "Why would you ask such a thing?"

"I don't know, this seemed like the time and place," said O'Brien.

"Unknowingly, you have touched upon a sore subject. My late wife had a firm belief that she was the reincarnation of one of the victims of the notorious Teardrop Killer."

O'Brien sat up straight. "Ooh! Is that what they called him?"

"My dear wife always felt, based on the content of her nightmares— if that is what we wish to call them—that the wrong man was blamed for those murders. She would say no more. It was a point of contention between us, her stubborn secrecy as to her personal revelations on the matter. Naturally, we do not like to be reminded of our petty squabbles with cherished ones who have departed. So you will forgive, I trust, this one lapse in my otherwise exhaustive catalog." Dr. Cherubino licked his long finger and flipped a few pages. "Here, for example, we find a series of incidents said to have occurred in this very house."

"Exciting," said O'Brien. She crossed her arms and rubbed them.

"Perhaps you would not think it so exciting were you Mr. Byron Welch, the previous owner of the property. He had no trouble for the first seven years he was living here, but then one summer night when the air conditioner was broken and he tossed and turned in his damp and sweltering bed, he heard a sound with which he was unfamiliar. Part of it was like a horse on cobblestones. Well, these were modern times, of course, and there were no horses to speak of in town, and certainly no cobblestones, and in any case the sound seemed to be coming from within the house. Beneath the clip-clop was a low whir or hum, almost a rumble. Taking the tenor part, if you will, came a high *tacka tacka tacka, tacka tacka tacka*. Mr. Welch was not a gambling man, but he did enjoy movies featuring high adventure in lavish settings, and to him this latter noise was reminiscent of a spinning roulette wheel with the bright little ball clattering among the grooves. *Tacka tacka tacka, tacka tacka tacka*. Was it the broken mechanism of the air conditioner, struggling to gain purchase? Byron Welch rose from the tangled counterpane and approached his bedroom window, outside of which the central cooling unit stood ruined and most silent. And still, from somewhere down the hall—from the room directly behind me this very instant, it so turned out, but more of that anon—came the unrelenting sound: *tacka tacka tacka. Tacka tacka tacka.*

"It so happened that some time prior to this occurrence, Mr. Welch had chanced upon a set of perfectly good golf clubs, it seemed to him, protruding somewhat obscenely from a trashcan on the street—his street, this street. One may conjecture about the amusing circumstances leading one of Mr. Welch's neighbors—or let us presume the *wife* of one of Mr. Welch's neighbors—to discard a set of golf clubs in such a fashion. But that is a story for another time, and for a decidedly more lighthearted anthology of domestic humor.

"Mr. Welch was not a golfer, but it seemed to him almost absurd not to avail himself of this peculiar and gratis merchandise. If he was not a golfer, nor was he a greedy man. He chose one club, one that appealed to him, an iron of pleasing heft and balance in his hands. He placed it by his bed, propped in the corner, and forgot about it. Only on the night in question did it occur to him that in its place and with its functional qualities the golf club might prove a protective instrument.

"The sound went on. *Tacka tacka tacka. Tacka tacka tacka.* Down the passageway stole Byron Welch, creeping stealthily, his trusty golf club raised as if to strike. When he put a toe on the threshold of this very room, the sound abruptly stopped. You may be sure Mr. Byron Welch assumed his cautious posture for several frozen minutes. But, for that night at least, the sound never returned. In spite of the swelter, Welch swore that a cold breeze passed over him, raising the goose flesh on his arms and legs.

"On Sundays, it was Mr. Welch's custom to perform the charitable act of driving a group of elderly women to the Baptist church, and afterward for a luncheon at Shoney's buffet restaurant in the neighboring town. It so happened that the incident in question had occurred on a Saturday night, so it was fresh in Welch's mind. He could hardly help chewing it over aloud to the sweet old women in his charge. They clucked and said, 'My, my,' but really didn't seem to pay it much mind, and eventually it passed from even his mind.

"After lunch he dropped off his ladies at their homes, one by one. At last there was just one passenger remaining, a Miss Grace Duncan, never married, who piped up from the back in her sweet voice, 'I know what you heard.'

"By this time, Byron Welch had nearly forgotten about the matter. 'What I heard?' he inquired. Miss Grace reminded him by making the sound: '*Tacka tacka tacka. Tacka tacka tacka,*' and somehow or another, a chill went up his spine. She just laughed, a tinkling, gay little laugh.

"'Why, dear,' she said. 'That's the sound of the treadle working on an old-fashioned sewing machine.'"

"Ooh, that gave me a shiver for some reason," said O'Brien.

Dr. Cherubino smiled with his long teeth. "Now, you may choose to believe that the old woman's passing comment acted as some sort of autosuggestion, coloring what happened next."

"May I interrupt you?" said O'Brien.

"I believe you have just taken that liberty," said Dr. Cherubino.

"I'm sorry, I couldn't hold my tongue any longer. I've been hit by an inspiration, and I don't want to let the moment go by. That's where the trouble always comes in for me: letting the moment go by. We really need to talk. This is lovely. I think I could get you some money for this, for your...work."

"Money?" said Dr. Cherubino. With a bang he shut the book.

"Yes, I happen to be looking for this kind of material right now. Well, not this specifically. I never would have dreamed of it. But now that I hear it, I completely see how I could use it."

"Use it?" Dr. Cherubino placed his palms on the cover of his black book. He placed them there with care, in the spirit of protection.

"I mean, you'd be cut in all the way, don't get me wrong. Let me explain." She jumped up and came toward him. By instinct, Dr. Cherubino hunched over his book, guarding it with his upper body. O'Brien backed off a little and Dr. Cherubino rose from his position almost sheepishly.

"Forgive me," he said.

"No, I completely understand," said O'Brien. "It's a personal project for you. You've put a lot of work into it. I'm just thinking of a way it could benefit the community and get in front of a lot more people, so you could enjoy the benefit of all the incredible work you've done. I've been called here to help revitalize the downtown area."

"That sounds terrible," said Dr. Cherubino.

"Not at all," said O'Brien. "Hear me out. My boyfriend and I were working for a big, important firm—"

"Boyfriend," said the bartender, mouth full of cracker.

"We wanted to get out on our own, hired guns, freelancers, consultants, see the country, bring big-city ideas to small communities in need. Plus which, my boyfriend was laid off and I quit in protest. It's an exciting time."

"Are you working for the Woodbines?" said Dr. Cherubino. The name seemed sour in his mouth.

"It doesn't matter who hired us," said O'Brien. "I'm working for the community. Now, what have you got going for you here? Not much, conventionally speaking. There's some morbid interest in the, what did you call it? The Teardrop Killer. There's a certain dark appeal to death tourism, sure. Did you know that the Lizzie Borden house is a bed and breakfast?"

"I shudder," said Dr. Cherubino.

"It's not for everybody. Or at least, not everybody wants to admit it. But what if we underplay it? People know about that part of the town's history, sure. What Smythe did with those industrial rolls of silk. It can be the hook, maybe. No pun intended. Because he also used a hook. We don't have to concentrate on the murders, not exclusively. We're inviting people to the Most Haunted Town in America. Isn't that what you said? Isn't that what you call it? Isn't that what it is?"

"I made some general remarks about the fifty-mile radius surrounding the bar," said Dr. Cherubino.

"Oh, details," said O'Brien.

"Many towns and cities claim to be the most haunted in America," said Dr. Cherubino. "Including St. Augustine, incredibly, which is balderdash. I admit that I've let the falsehoods of such feckless city fathers rankle me, and sometimes at night, abed, I have considered what steps I might take to correct the rampant misinformation, the sloppy guesswork that passes for statistics in paranormal circles, the lack of regard for serious research. Were I to compose a stern form letter to various chambers of commerce, would that be just my human vainglory talking?"

"Oh, I don't think so, sir," said O'Brien. "I think you have to stand up for what you believe in. You're already a local celebrity. I think you could be a national one. I see you leading tours, acting as a spokesman for the town. I see a school dedicated to the study of the ghostly sciences, with you as the dean in a special robe. I see a series of TV movies stimulating the local economy, shot on the sites of the actual events. My BF is a respected DP."

"And my uncle was a world-class dipsomaniac," said Dr. Cherubino. "Is. He is still with us at a hundred and ten, and so many of his betters cold in the ground. I am sorry. This is all so overwhelming. I wish there were a way to consult with my late wife."

"Isn't there?" said O'Brien.

"I have never had much luck."

"Those things are evil," said the bartender through another mouthful of cheese and crackers. "Ouija boards."

"My Julia would have agreed with you. Some things stand out in my memory, chiefly the amazing speed with which the phrase 'yellow fever' was spelled out. The planchette fairly flew from our hands."

"I have one," said the bartender. "My great-aunt and uncle, this was her second husband, she met him in the Army. Well, they broke off from the Baptist church because she started speaking in tongues. One day she just started speaking in tongues and the deacons didn't like it. And my great-aunt, you know, she's pretty stubborn, so she's like, 'Fine! I'll start my own church.' So there was this preacher that was coming through town, one of these revivalists with the tents, they were going to set up out there behind the old fruit stand. You know that place. What it had for a roof was this huge slanting sheet of rusted-out metal that used to be the back of the screen for the drive-in movie. That's all gone now. You remember the old fruit stand, Doc?"

"I do not," said the doctor.

"Maybe I'm not describing it right. The front of the fruit stand was the *back* of the old drive-in movie screen. Is this ringing a bell?"

"I fear not," said the doctor.

"You'd drive about two miles out of town and oh, never mind. It's gone now anyway. Anyhow, nobody wanted this traveling preacher around. He was supposed to look like a praying mantis. Now, you're not going to believe what happened next. It just may chill and surprise you."

Dr. Cherubino took up his conversation with O'Brien again, as if the bartender weren't there. "I must have some assurances if we are to continue any sort of discussion. My work is important to me."

"Of course," said O'Brien. "And I'd never use any of it without permission, if that's what you're worried about. Is that why you're worried, Dr. Cherubino?"

"How did you know my name?"

"Oh! This guy told me."

"Bill Dawes," said the bartender.

"Is that your name?" asked O'Brien.

"Bill Dawes," said the bartender.

Dr. Cherubino seemed to be considering many things. Finally, he spoke. "During my time in Greece I belonged to a secret society of thirteen individuals, each of us with a different talent. Are either of you familiar with tyromancy?"

O'Brien and Bill Dawes said they were unfamiliar with tyromancy.

"It is the telling of fortunes through the medium of cheese. Each tyromancer possesses his own peculiar methodology. One, for example, might have a rat as a familiar. The answer is given according to which cube of cheese the rat decides to eat."

"Like throwing the I Ching," said O'Brien.

"A fascinating comparison, and not an altogether ludicrous one. Yes, you intrigue me. I am inclined to trust you, young lady. In so many ways you bring to mind my Julia. The fact remains, however, that I am not able to consult oracularly on the matter as I would like. You have eaten all the cheese."

"Sorry," said Bill Dawes.

"No apology necessary. As your host, I provided it to be eaten, along with these delicious crackers from Israel. I had not considered that tyromancy might be required this evening. Truth be told, I seldom have occasion to practice that art any longer. It is a lonely business, practicing tyromancy for one's self."

"Do you want me to run out and get some more cheese?" said Bill Dawes. He took his mulberry Goober hat off his knee, placed it on his head, and rose.

"The cheese I require must be ordered specially through the mail services," said Dr. Cherubino.

"Well, that was some good cheese," said Bill Dawes.

"I didn't get any," said O'Brien.

"I'm a pig," said Bill Dawes. "Hey, so do you want to hear about my cousin that threw up a demon or not?"

"We do not," said Dr. Cherubino.

"Huh," said Bill Dawes.

Dr. Cherubino took Bill Dawes's vacated spot on the loveseat and motioned for O'Brien. She sat down next to him. He looked into O'Brien's eyes.

"What I propose is a test," he said. "I will tell you the story of 'The Black Parasol.' If you can bear to hear it from beginning to end without going mad, without screaming or begging me to stop or fleeing this house in terror, I will give serious consideration to your business proposal."

"Sounds great," said O'Brien.

"I need to use the can," said Bill Dawes.

"All the way down the hall, to the left," said Dr. Cherubino. "Please use the latch or the door will spring open on you while you are attempting to conduct your business."

"The haunted toilet," said Bill Dawes.

"Merely inadequate carpentry, I fear," said Dr. Cherubino.

He watched Bill Dawes disappear down the dark hall before turning back to O'Brien.

"The facts of the case are well-known," said Dr. Cherubino. "I mean, of course, the mundane, earthly facts. The fire occurred in 1885. I have all the clippings, the eyewitness accounts. The house of the Black Parasol stood on the corner of Hellman and Magnolia, which you must have passed on the way here. The lot contains the shuttered remnants of a gas station and convenience store."

"I don't remember," said O'Brien.

"No matter. At the time of which we are speaking, it held a rambling, almost ludicrous structure, a prominent boarding house with a few unusual features. For one thing, the house was built directly onto the street. That is, there was no lawn. The immense boarding house was immediately accessible from Magnolia and took up a great deal of the lot. The family who owned and ran it were..." He gave her a look. "*Woodbines.* Mr. Woodbine was an older gentleman. His wife was some years younger but had never given him offspring. It was widely suggested that she *could* not. They had, however, adopted a young ward, Marcella by name, who, at the time of our story, was seventeen years old and to be married the following month. Now, I must tell you that another unusual feature of the boarding house was that the Woodbines had given over a portion of the ground floor to a lazy young grocer, who set up a small shop there."

Dr, Cherubino was silent for a moment. He looked troubled.

"I will ask you once more. Are you acquainted with the Woodbines?" he said.

"Um…no?"

He looked at her.

"They're a local family, I guess?" said O'Brien. "Important? Wealthy?"

"Yes, important and wealthy and powerful, and they do not appreciate the story I am telling you now."

"Got it," she said.

"The Crowns, to which my own Julia was related, are the true old family of Ordain, as regal as their name. A Woodbine won't deign to hear of them. The Woodbines began as pretenders and, some would say, continue along that line. Crown is still a first or middle name hereabouts, but for two generations now no descendent of a Crown has given birth to a male heir. That is the Curse of the Crowns, well known. Though the remaining Crown sisters strongly identify themselves as such, the actual surname has evaporated—a wisp, a whisper, a ghost—whereas the Woodbines remain hearty and pervasive as weeds. Though his fellows be mowed down like blades of grass, a Woodbine sprouts his head from any tragedy, as my story will attest. For you see, the shiftless young grocer was Cullen Woodbine, or so he fashioned himself, who just showed up in town one day, supposedly the son of the elder Woodbine from a previous marriage. Some say that Cullen Woodbine was in reality a no-account bastard from God knows where, if you will forgive me.

"Young Cullen Woodbine maintained sleeping quarters at the house in addition to his little business. The source of the fire appears to have been a twenty-gallon can of kerosene belonging to him. How it came to be ignited is a mystery, if not much of one. Woodbine gave his account to the local paper, preemptively and rapidly, it strikes me. He had a theatrical engagement and asked his mysterious friend Sidney to watch the store in his absence. A theatrical engagement! Even in those more cultured times a curious alibi for this part of the state. Upon Cullen's return, around midnight, he convinced the fellow Sidney, about whom not much is known, to stay over. They lay awake for the space of a half hour, talking amiably before succumbing to slumber. And now I will quote Cullen Woodbine's public statement: 'While we were talking we heard Miss Marcella overhead running her sewing machine. She generally sewed until a late hour, as she was to be married on February sixteenth, and was making her trousseau.'"

"Sewing," said O'Brien.

"Indeed," said Dr. Cherubino. "I have contemplated that very recurrence and considered the mythologies linking needlework to the raveling or unraveling of fate."

Dr. Cherubino told O'Brien all about how Cullen Woodbine and his friend Sidney had drifted to sleep. The next thing Cullen knew, he told the newspaper, "I was startled from my sleep and found the bed on which I was sleeping enveloped by flames. I sprang from my bed and met my father in my room. I said, 'My God, where is Miss Marcella?'"

In his accounting, Cullen Woodbine made himself out to be quite the hero, braving the flaming staircase in vain, assisting in various rescues of other tenants, at last fainting from the heat and smoke. The town constable, however, passed on a different story to the same reporter, having spoken with this Sidney, who had seen Cullen Woodbine earlier that evening, putting away a large box of matches.

Cullen had asked him if he were hard to wake, and Sidney answered that he was. The next thing he recollected was Cullen whispering in his ear, asking him if he didn't think something was the matter.

Dr. Cherubino, who had been telling his story with his eyes closed for some time, opened them.

"Whispering in his ear," he said. "Didn't he think something was the matter. Is he hard to wake. What was Cullen's true relationship with Miss Marcella, by every normal societal measure his sister? But I go too far. Most prosaically, and with an old-fashioned good sense that may prove our best ally here, a final note in the paper informs us that Cullen Woodbine's stock of groceries was insured at the princely sum of four hundred and fifty dollars.

"'Notwithstanding the promptness of the firemen, the building was consumed, and at the same time, two persons.' Ah. An elegance lacking in the tabloids of today. Mrs. Woodbine, having broken her thigh in a fall some weeks before the tragedy, was helpless, and perished. Likewise our Marcella. And here is where our story begins."

"Wow," said O'Brien. "Seems like it began a lot already, but okay."

"We must forgive our ancestors. They were bereft of entertainment. Have you ever witnessed a person playing the spoons?"

"There was a Soundgarden video my brother loved," said O'Brien.

"I have no idea what that means, nor do I wish to," said Dr. Cherubino. "But I will ask you to imagine a world in which playing the spoons—slapping a pair of spoons on one's knee or thereabouts—was the pinnacle of artistic achievement, as it certainly was in Ordain. For all I know, that may have been the nature of Woodbine's theatrical engagement. We cannot fault the morbid turn that the curiosity of our own citizens took in the days after the fire. A certain Miss Isobel Hayes received a sealed letter from her beau, asking her to meet him at the site of the terrible fire well after curfew. There was to be a bright moon and I suppose the fellow had some Byronic pretensions, in love with the beauty of decay and ruin, or perhaps he fancied himself a Mississippi Baudelaire. In any case, Miss Hayes was properly titillated. She arrived as requested at the still-smoldering remains of the once-great house. Somewhere, a fox cried—the cry of the vixen, like a woman's shrieking. Miss Hayes drew her shawl about her and called out to her beau. There came no answer. She had a mind to run back home, but as she turned to go the glint of the moon fell on some treasure. Thrilling to a wicked shock of avarice and taboo, Isobel Hayes stepped into the wreckage.

"Waiting for her was a curious object like a long bone, lying in a rapturous fan of what she took to be the most exquisite lace, blackened by flame. It was, she thought, the remnant of a fine lady's parasol, a worthy souvenir. Imbedded in the handle of the black parasol was what seemed to be large, glittering red jewel. When she went to retrieve her prize, the lovely lacework fell away and disintegrated. Now her wonderful parasol was no better than a black stick, gritty to the touch and giving off an odor of smoky rot. She dropped it, repelled. Yet still the great gem winked at her. No matter how she tried, she could not pry it from the stalk that clasped it tight. And how she tried. Squatting there like a mad-woman or an animal, this prim specimen, this beloved Sunday school teacher, growled and salivated with the effort. A domestic sound—the glassy congress of two milk bottles, say, or the mewl-ing of a hungry infant; why not the crowing of a cock, dazzled by the burning moon?—restored her to her senses. She perceived her ashy crinoline. Miss Hayes hopped up and ran home, as you may imagine, suddenly no more than a scared little girl.

"You may imagine as well her horror when she arrived at her little room to strip away her dirty garments and cleanse her tainted soul, only to discover what she had carried with her, gripped in her fist, the entire way home unawares. Of course, it was the handle of the terrible black parasol. With a scream stifled by the dainty heel of her palm so as not to wake her parents, she banished the dreaded thing at once to the backmost part of her chifforobe, intending to return it to its proper resting place, the remains of the Woodbine boarding house, come the morning. She latched the door of the chifforobe and leaned a chair against it as a superstitious precaution. A few bitter drops of her mother's laudanum helped Miss Hayes at last to sleep, until the softest sound awakened her: the gentle *creak-creak-creaking* of the chifforobe door.

"It was the peculiar habit of Miss Hayes to sleep with several pillows at her back, in a half-sitting position, so that all she had to do was open her eyes to see what lay across the room from her, the coursing moonlight lying in slashes upon it. The door of the chifforobe was hanging open, as was the mouth of poor Marcella, who hung in the air, whole and pale while her charred dressing gown blew in tatters, a living orange spark dancing here and there on sleeve or hem, her virginal body exposed, her virtuous face stretched out in an obscene parody of melancholy, as if she meant to speak in confidence to her bosom friend, her little Isobel, once again, the sad eyes of the phantom Marcella bubbling like gelatin, her sweet mouth a black hole, ringed by black teeth, and from the loathsome flickering of her huge and blackened tongue there issued forth a most unholy sound…"

All at once a violent shaking rocked them, a high-pitched, threatening, skeletal clatter that seemed to come from everywhere.

Dr. Cherubino clutched his chest and cried mercy.

O'Brien screamed and screamed. Dr. Cherubino fell forward onto her and she shoved him off. She got up and ran down the hallway, screaming. It was dark and she smashed into a pile of books, bloodying her knee.

The back door burst open and O'Brien thought she might swoon. She had never swooned nor fainted but suddenly she understood the feeling.

There was Bill Dawes, standing in the kitchen, laughing.

"Did I get y'all?" he said. "I guess I did!" He laughed some more.

"Get us?" screamed O'Brien. She ran toward him with her hand upraised. "Get us? You're a bad person!"

"Aw, I just rattled the screen a little. Like a campfire surprise."

He held her arm so she couldn't slap him. She relented.

"I'm pregnant, you asshole!" she said.

"I served you drinks!" he screamed.

"Bitters and soda."

"White wine spritzers!"

"I only finished one."

"Bitters are like forty-five percent alcohol!"

"They are?" She was thinking about how you only used a few drops of bitters in anything, and was about to say it, when they noticed how quiet the house had become.

They found Dr. Cherubino dead. He lay on his back, eyes and mouth wide. His hair had turned quite white, and was dotted profanely with cracker crumbs. On the podium rested his book, filled from front to back, as the county sheriff would soon discover, with nothing but miniscule geometric symbols that only Dr. Cherubino could have read.

Art Is the Most Important Thing

HIS WIFE WAS CALLING.

"Your home phone isn't working," she said.

"A lot of people don't even have landlines anymore," said Cookie.

"But you do," said his wife.

"The power is out," said Cookie. "The lines are down, or whatever they have now. Do they still have lines? I'm not doing anything."

"You're slurring your words," said his wife.

"How can you tell?" said Cookie. He whispered to Sandy: "I'm going to step out on the porch."

"Who are you talking to?" said his wife.

"Myself," said Cookie.

He was dashing off so quickly that he had already opened the back door. The rain had died down. Everything was dark and smelled good.

"I think I just let a fly in the house," said Cookie.

"I'm sorry. Listen, I wrote a book-length poem."

"That's great!" said Cookie.

"…about the dissolution of our marriage."

"Today I saw a bumblebee in the clover," said Cookie.

"Did you hear me? I wrote a book-length poem about the dissolution of our marriage."

"Why don't you fax it over?" said Cookie.

"What do you mean? Do you have a fax machine?"

"No. I was casting about for something to say."

"And the lines are down anyway."

"Art is the most important thing," said Cookie.

"Right?" said his wife.

They laughed.

Duck Call Gang

You should try sitting in your house in the dark listening to some troubled youths blow on their duck calls outside your window. It happens to me sometimes when my wife has gone to bed and I am staying up late, accompanied by my insomnia and worries about the future. I turn off the TV and stand there trembling in the dark and work up my courage to part the curtains just enough to see the lanky toughs there dimly through the fog, standing in the road and blowing their duck calls for no discernable reason. What are they up to? They seem like the kind of churls who would pull a cat's tail for their idea of fun. I worry about all the little cats out there in the world.

I am not yet what you would call an old man, but it is only a matter of time. For the present, I feel I could beat up one young person if need be, in the defense of my wife, my cats, my home. Were there two young people, however, I might have more trouble, as one of them held my arms behind my back while the other scoffed openly at me and struck me repeatedly in the solar plexus, for example. Maybe a third is forcing my wife to watch. Most horrible!

Lightning struck our house the other night. It woke us from our slumber. We woke up screaming. The lightning knocked a painting off the wall and broke its frame and messed up the computer, though not irreparably, and that seemed to be the extent of the damage. Afterward, we lay there in the dark and began to laugh. We laughed at ourselves and one another, at the quality of our screaming. I cannot recall ever having screamed in actual terror before. I was relieved not to have suffered a heart attack.

Now one of the cats, formerly the bravest of our crew, crawls under the covers next to me whenever there is a thunderstorm in the middle of the night. Poor thing!

"Couple Killed in Metal Bed," was one remark I tossed off lightly, pretending to quote a headline in the next morning's paper. Our dark humor. Our bed is an old iron thing that belonged to an ancestor who was not a wealthy man. We see its like in movies about corrupt orphanages or old-time sanitariums. Our style of bed is associated with the misery rampant in the most venal institutions of yore.

After our laughter subsided, I lay there, still wide awake, long after my wife's gentle breathing once again suggested untroubled sleep, and then I entertained my anxious thoughts, such as, "If we had been screaming tonight at the approach of a masked serial murderer, no one would have heard us scream."

Yes, who will take care of us when we are old?

Our children? We have no children. Of course, having children is no guarantee of anything. Even the best parent may produce an ungrateful child. I myself have been an ungrateful child.

Our cats will not take care of us when we are old. That is not their job, although cats are handed out to patients in dank retirement homes for the warmth and affection they provide.

Should my wife and I perish in our home, crushed under old newspapers or merely by old age, our cats might be forced to feed on our corpses, which is perfectly acceptable. When someone kicks in the door because we haven't been heard from for several days, the cats might be right there on top of us, turning their heads from our bodies and toward the sound. Our tardy rescuer will be startled by the glistening crimson in which their muzzles are drenched.

Will we take care of one another, my wife and I? Once I fell out of the shower and hit the back of my head on the toilet. Although my wife was nearby, sneaking a cigarette on the porch, she did not hear the crash, and I lay there for several moments alone.

Before it is too late we should find an apprentice, someone to whom we can introduce all the finer things in life, such as caviar—a disadvantaged teen who will beam with gratitude and drive us to the grocery store when we become too feeble to see. It dawns on me that I will pluck this individual from the ranks of the Duck Call Gang itself.

I know there is a fable about suckling a viper at your bosom, but I can't recall whether it is pro or con. Night is coming, and the thing to do is hope for the best.